The Bloody Key

A Bluebeard Retelling

L.J. Thomas

Forestedge Press

First Edition: April 2023

Forestedge Press

Cover illustration by Elaine Ho | artofelaineho.com

Cover design by Mallory Rock | rocksolidbookdesign.com

Copy Editing by Vicky Brewster | vickybrewstereditor.com

The Bloody Key

ISBN 978-1-7332610-4-3 (Paperback)

ISBN 978-1-7332610-3-6 (eBook)

www.ljthomasbooks.com

To my parents,
who inspired my love of reading
and filled our home with books—
including a beautifully illustrated one
full of magical, kid-friendly fairy tales,
and which also included . . . Bluebeard

For there is no friend like a sister
In calm or stormy weather;
To cheer one on the tedious way,
To fetch one if one goes astray,
To lift one if one totters down,
To strengthen whilst one stands.
— Christina Rossetti, "Goblin Market"

Editor's Note

W hat follows is an account of the extraordinary events
that occurred at Tiefenwald Castle
in the 24th Year of the Reign of King Lukas IV,
compiled from the surviving letters and diaries
of those who lived within its accursed walls.

CHAPTER ONE

Anne's Diary

7 AUGUST

We met a man in the meadow today.

It was like something from one of my favorite stories, those in which an encounter with a mysterious stranger upends someone's life. Liesl and I have told many such stories while spending balmy afternoons tending our goats, dreaming of hidden worlds and far-flung adventures. Before today, I never imagined we'd meet such a stranger—someone who could change our fortunes or twist our fates.

Liesl and I had decided to weave flower crowns for each other while the goats idly grazed. We sat in the shade of our favorite twisted oak tree after gathering the wildflowers. They grew thick this late in the summer, sweetening the air with their perfume and splashing color across the green hills, stretching out to the distant mountains.

I'd woven Liesl's crown quickly, so she was wearing it when the stranger approached. My half-finished crown was still clasped in her hands. She is a better weaver than me, but it takes her longer, as she chooses each flower carefully, according to a sense about which colors and sizes look well together that I do not have.

The man approached us on a beautiful white stallion—the sort that only the very rich keep. It had as little in common with our tired brown plow horse as a swan does a sparrow.

"Remember to curtsy, Anne," Liesl said, pulling me to my feet and smoothing her dark hair.

As he neared, I could see that the man's clothing, too, was of the finest sort. I wondered how far he had traveled in them. The velvets and silks would surely not hold up to more than a few days on horseback along our dusty and uneven roads. Perhaps he was so rich that it did not matter if his clothing wore out so soon.

My own dress was a few years old, the elbows patched and the hem rather short now. As I admired the man, I suddenly felt ungainly in my ill-fitting dress and childish to be making flower crowns—something I had never felt before. Perhaps Liesl felt it, too, as her cheeks turned rather pink.

Smiling, he dismounted his horse to speak to us. For one moment, I had the urge to run—I know not why. It vanished as he said in a deep voice, "Good day, Frauleins," and doffed his brown felt hat. A long black feather—from a raven, perhaps—stuck out from its brim.

We curtsied. Liesl dropped my unfinished flower crown in the dirt but seemed to forget about the one she wore. I looked to her for guidance, and she said to the man, "Good day, my liege. How may we serve you?"

He didn't reply right away. I suppose he was studying us as we studied him. He was older than I had at first thought, with lines around his mouth and the corners of his eyes. Perhaps my father's age, though he moved with the energy of a much younger man. He was rather round about the middle, I suspect because he could partake in rich food and wine just as he did in expensive fabrics.

The most striking thing, however—the thing that most drew the eye and made taking the whole of him in at once difficult—was his long blue beard.

It was not blue in the way that the sky or the forget-me-nots in the meadow are blue, but rather in the way that some of our goats are "red." Their coats are black as can be in the shade, but when the sun hits them, more fiery tones are revealed.

The sun was high today in the meadow, and the stranger's hair and beard shone remarkably blue. He was no wizard or warlock, of course, but it gave him a touch of the otherworldly. I didn't mean to stare, but I must have, for he said, "Ah, Fraulein, I see you've observed my most unique feature, and the one for which I am named. I am lord of a castle a few days' travel from here and in possession of a slew of grandiose names, but everyone knows me as Bluebeard. You may address me so, too. Now, what might I call you?"

His gallant manner was so different from those of the men in our village, yet it was far from the reserved, imperious way that we had heard other nobles speak on the rare occasions we'd encountered any.

"My name is Liesl, and this is my younger sister, Anne." Liesl smoothed her skirts and touched her flower crown self-consciously, as if she'd just remembered it. For a moment, I thought she might take the white-and-blue flowers from her head and drop them beside my crown in the dirt, but she clasped her hands in front of her instead.

"Well met, Liesl and Anne."

"You have a lovely horse," I said, then chided myself for saying something so inane.

His eyes flicked to me, and he nodded with a little smile before returning his attention back to Liesl. "Is there an inn nearby? I desire a hot meal and a soft bed."

Liesl described the location of the village inn, though I expected he would be disappointed with its meager offerings. Bluebeard thanked us, remounted his horse, and gave us one last appraising look before turning back onto the road.

Neither Liesl nor I spoke of the stranger after he left, though she took off her flower crown and never finished mine. When we brought the goats home, I hurried to record our meeting with Bluebeard before I forgot any details. I'd been saving this diary for months—Warner gave it to me for my last birthday, and I was afraid to touch a pen to its pages, not wanting to waste it on anything inconsequential. Now, of course, I worry that is exactly what I have done.

I had thought our silence was because Liesl and I both felt the strange weight of the exchange, the way it had felt like a *beginning*. The way his riches and unsettling beard felt like something from one of our stories. But now that I've written of it, I doubt myself; perhaps she said nothing of it because it meant so little. Certainly, for a lord such as him, it must have been but one uneventful moment like a thousand others he has had while riding across the land. It would not seem so fraught with meaning or change as it did to me. Oh, the marvelous things he must have seen, and how little I have.

But still, whenever I remember his gaze on me, my face flushes and something turns, low in my belly.

CHAPTER TWO

Bluebeard's Diary

7 AUGUST

N ever again, I had told myself after Amalie. But had I not said this before? As Cacilie died in my arms, I swore I would not love again. But there were others, in time. One and all, they betrayed me and left me to live alone.

I'd been on my own for many years before her, but I had been sure about Amalie. I had known she would be the one to grow old with me. A placid little thing who never raised her voice. As beautiful as all the others, but more likely to be found curled by the fire in winter, head bent over some detailed embroidery work. Even in the summer, she rarely left sight of the castle.

And yet she, too, had failed me.

I should give up on this endeavor altogether, forsake ever finding love, someone whose life I wished to share. I all but had.

But then—Liesl and her sister Anne. Sitting in the meadow, the wind lifting their hair and tightening their linen dresses against their newly blossomed forms.

The thought struck me that I had not tried this avenue yet. No peasant girls were among my past loves, and perhaps that had been my mistake. A girl who sat in muddy fields and tended goats would be dazzled by my rich halls, would not ask the questions she should not dare. She would obey.

I approached on my horse—the white one, luckily, to cast me in the role of a gallant knight—and introduced myself to the girls. I saw my effect on them, and, also, that they were both worth seeing. The freckled girl was more young than beautiful, perhaps, but with the right dresses and accoutrements, she could look well on my arm. The elder sister, though, truly had something. Raven hair, a swan-like neck, a bashful pink blush across her creamy skin when I spoke to her.

Yes. She will do nicely.

One with an open heart like mine, and a castle so empty but for the ghosts, must do what is right and necessary.

It is time to love again.

CHAPTER THREE

Anne's Diary

8 AUGUST

As it turns out, I am not foolish at all. Oh, I am wise, wise, because Bluebeard returned today!

Klaus alerted me to his visit. I was milking one of our goats in the barn when he hurried out to fetch me. "Annie," he said, rushing in and nearly overturning the milk pail. "Come inside at once. A man is here—a nobleman."

My hand froze on the bucket. I was so surprised I didn't even complain, the way I usually do, that I haven't gone by "Annie" since I was a child.

"What did he look like?" I asked.

"A very long beard, and he's dressed quite well. He rode a white horse."

My pulse raced, but I blew a strand of hair from my face as I continued to milk the nanny goat. "We saw him yesterday, in the meadow."

"You did? Why didn't you say anything?"

I caught the tone of hurt in his voice, even as he fidgeted with anticipation. Only a year and a half older than me—and two years younger than Liesl—Klaus had always been our favorite brother, and he was used to me telling him everything. But I'd felt silly after writing of the encounter in my diary and so had said nothing of Bluebeard. I couldn't believe he'd come to the house because of *us*—it must have been a coincidence—but Klaus's enthusiasm was catching.

"He only asked us for directions. I didn't think he would return."

Klaus took my hands and pulled me to my feet. "Well, he has, and he said he's looking for a wife."

"What does that have to do with us? He's a nobleman."

"You must come inside. Though he hasn't yet said as much, I suspect he means to ask Father to marry one of you." He frowned at my appearance, straightening my apron and pushing loose strands of hair behind my ears.

I pushed him away. "Do stop, Klaus. What am I, a goat you're readying for market?" But my annoyance masked a sharp pang of anxiety. I was right yesterday when I felt that my life was on the edge of change. Now that it was here, I didn't feel at all ready for it. I knew one thing, though: Klaus must be mistaken as to why Bluebeard had come. A man with his wealth surely would not want a goatherd for a wife.

"Hurry, now," Klaus said, shifting his weight from foot to foot.

"Very well," I said, as I'd just finished with the milking anyway. I brushed out my skirts, retied the kerchief around my hair, and hoisted the milk pail. We stepped into the bright summer sun, and Klaus hurried me around our flock of chickens and into the house.

Inside, my father and Bluebeard sat at our wooden table, flagons of ale between them. Liesl had abandoned the spinning wheel she'd worked at all day and stood quietly in the corner, hands clasped and eyes down demurely. Careful not to spill any milk and conscious of the stranger's eyes on me, I set the pail next to the basket of wool and took my place beside my older sister. I tried my best to look as ladylike as she did, but it was difficult with my unsettled thoughts and pounding heart. Bluebeard must have worn a heavy cologne of some kind, one that mixed oddly with the usual cedar scent of our walls, and I felt the beginnings of a headache.

"Ah, there's your other lovely daughter," Bluebeard said, and I glanced up quickly. His eyes glinted in the scant light through the window. I wondered if he remembered my name.

My father watched Bluebeard study the two of us. "How may I help with your quest for a wife, my liege?" he asked.

"Yesterday, I traveled near your home, and your girls were kind enough to point me on my way. I've been thinking of their lovely faces ever since."

Out of the corner of my eye, I saw Liesl blush and smile bashfully. I was too nervous to be pleased by his compliments. I still had that same unsettled feeling from yesterday, and for a moment, the sharp metal taste of fear filled my mouth. Perhaps it was only a little cowardice at the thought of leaving my home and family.

Father inclined his head. "So you've said, my liege."

"It is not good for a man to be alone," Bluebeard declared, holding his mug aloft, then gulping down half the ale. He wiped his mouth on his shirt, and I had to hide my dismay at his carelessness with such fine fabric. "I'm sure you know that, my good man. Is your wife out with the goats today?"

"My wife," Father began, then cleared his throat. "My wife, God rest her soul, has been gone these ten years, my liege. But I have not been alone. Blessed with seven children, my life cannot be anything but full."

"Of course, of course, my good man. I see your family, and I admit I am jealous. I have no children, and I lost my last wife fifteen years ago this October. It has been rather lonesome since then." He paused to take another swig of ale.

Father wrapped his hands around his own mug. "I'm afraid, my liege, I still don't see how I can help you."

Bluebeard continued as if he hadn't spoken. "I'd rather thought to be done with the whole marriage business, old as I am now, and broken as my heart was after the loss of my last wife. But yesterday, I saw your girls in the meadow, and I thought of how much more of a *home* my castle might seem with a wife like one of your daughters."

I inhaled sharply before I could stop myself, but he didn't seem to mind. In fact, a broad grin stretched over his face.

"You cannot mean this, my liege. Do be serious," my father replied in a steady voice. I agreed with him—a nobleman needed a wife of his own class. Someone who knew how to keep a castle and wear fancy hairstyles and dresses, or whatever it is noblewomen do.

"I am serious as the grave," Bluebeard said. "And I aim to stay here a few weeks so I may woo one of your daughters and show you how well I can provide for her. For the whole family—I could, of course, arrange a generous stipend."

My father shook his head and clasped his hands tighter around the flagon. "I'm sorry, my liege, but I don't think I could do without either of my daughters. And they are yet so young. Liesl is just nineteen, and Anne is not yet sixtee—"

"Nonsense. I daresay they are both of marriageable age. Give it a fortnight and we shall see what they think, my good man."

For the first time since I had entered, Father looked at us. His face was lined with worry, the set of his mouth resigned. My skin felt tight over my heart. Bluebeard is a noble, and we are only simple farmers and goatherds—I'm not sure my father could defy him even if he desperately wanted to. Klaus stood back in the opposite corner, crossing and uncrossing his arms, his expression unreadable.

"My girls," Father said. "What do you say to this man's proposal?"

Luckily, Liesl spoke while I was still trying to determine whether I dared decline a nobleman's request. "I would welcome his attentions, Father," she said, then gave Bluebeard a coy smile. "Though I must warn him that I am not easily wooed. I dearly love our farm and my family and would be giving up a great deal to be wed to him."

After a tense pause, Bluebeard guffawed and slapped his knee. "You see, my good man? She is old enough to know her own mind."

My father barely hid his grimace, then looked at me with kind eyes. "And you, Anne?"

I swallowed. What was Liesl doing? Did she *want* to be taken away from us, to leave with this stranger? I suppose a small part of me wanted the rich comfort of a castle, to live out one of my favorite fairy tales. A larger part of me trembled to think of being married to this man. But I trusted my sister to know what was best. "I feel the same as Liesl," I finally managed to say.

"It's settled then," Bluebeard said. His chair scraped along the packed-earth floor as he stood and clasped my father's hand. "Thank you for the ale, my good man. My campaign for one of your daughter's hearts shall begin the day after tomorrow, with a dance in the town square."

Liesl smiled prettily, and he gave her a long look—one I might describe as *hungry*—before grinning at me, then donning his cap and leaving our home.

And so, in two days, the wooing shall commence.

Chapter Four

Anne's Diary

9 August

None of us are quite sure if Bluebeard will carry through on his plans to court us. Perhaps he stopped by on a whim and has no intention of pursuing us further. Or perhaps he will see sense and seek a wife among his own kind. Surely with all the noblewomen of Westenfall at his disposal, he does not need to stoop to Liesl or me.

But in case he is serious about us, Father gave Liesl and I each a few coins so we could go into town and find things with which to freshen up our appearances. It was not enough to buy new fabric, nor would we have time to sew any new garments, but we planned to get new hair ribbons or buttons or perhaps a bit of lace with which to retrim our dresses.

It did not take long at the milliner's, as we had so little to spend, and I deferred to Liesl's judgment about which scraps of finery would best improve my shabby dresses. Then we journeyed over to the printshop.

Nearly ten years ago, Warner, the eldest of our siblings, left home to become an apprentice with the town booksmith and printshop owner. Five years ago, he married the booksmith's lovely daughter, Silvia, whom Liesl and I were overjoyed to welcome as our sister. Warner was the first to leave home, but he was followed by Gerard, who works the stables of a local merchant, training horses. Heller is itching to move out next, but so far, has not found a position that will allow him to leave.

As we entered, I breathed in the comforting scent of the workshop. Ink and old paper and book bindings. Warner was bent over the old illuminated manuscript he has been restoring, but he greeted us with a smile and then one of his bear hugs.

"I hear I'm to congratulate one of you on a rather exciting suitor," Warner said, grinning.

Liesl smiled and arched an eyebrow. "Let's not count our chickens before they hatch."

"And what do you think, Annie?" he asked, poking me in the side. "Are you ready to walk down the aisle to a lord?"

My face heated to the tips of my ears. I found my tongue tied, only managing to stammer, "Well, I—"

Silvia swept down the stairs then, tsking. "Come, darling, don't frighten your poor little sister." She kissed him on the cheek, patted his chest, and turned to us. "No more of this teasing. Do you two have time to chat in all this excitement?"

Liesl assured her we did, and Silvia ushered us up to the apartment above the shop for tea.

We settled into the timeworn upholstered chairs as Silvia poured tea into elegant-but-chipped little cups. After the usual niceties and compliments on her lemon cakes, Silvia smiled and congratulated us on our good fortune.

"I knew it was only a matter of time before someone better than that butcher's boy would spot you," she said to Liesl. "And Anne, too. I hear the lord had compliments for you as well."

"His eyes were all for Liesl." I tried not to sound too relieved.

"I heard he has been making calls all over town—to the baker and florist and musicians. We're all in for quite a celebration tomorrow."

I set my teacup back in its saucer with a clink. "So he has been planning? He really means to carry this through?"

"All signs seem to indicate so," Silvia said. Light spilled through the lace curtains over the windows, drawing attention to her straw-pale hair and dark blue eyes.

I'd always admired Silvia. She is lovely and kind and knows more about the printing press than even my brother. She is so comfortable in her home and her role as my brother's wife. I don't imagine myself ever fitting anywhere so snugly. Especially not with someone like Bluebeard.

Liesl sipped her tea delicately. Fighting off a smile, she said, "It would be an advantageous match for our family."

Silvia took a dainty bite of a lemon cake and patted her lips with a napkin. "Do you know anything about this . . . Bluebeard?"

"Has his name spread so far already?" Liesl asked, laughing.

"You know how Coesfeld is."

Liesl leaned forward and smiled conspiratorially. "And what do the good people of Coesfeld know about him?"

"Rather little, I'm afraid." Silvia set her empty plate on the little table. I realized I hadn't touched my lemon cake yet, then panicked and took a bite so big that Liesl frowned at me. Silvia lowered her voice and said, "He's known to be a wealthy widower who owns Tiefenwald Castle—an old, stately affair four days' ride from here."

Waving a hand, Liesl said, "Yes, yes, we know all that. What *else* do they say?"

"Well," Silvia said, pursing her lips momentarily, "there is some gossip. Something to do with his wife—it was nearly fifteen years ago, so who can say what really happened? But there are rumors she ran away."

"Really?" Liesl asked. A crease formed between her eyebrows.

My hands began to sweat, and I set the remains of my lemon cake on the table. I wanted nothing to do with a middle-aged nobleman who'd scared off his last wife.

I got up and walked to the window. On the street below, I saw a small band of villagers chatting and sneaking glances up at the shop. Frau Frida was among them. The lacy curtains shielded me from their view, but clearly they'd seen Liesl and me stop by, and we were their subject of conversation.

"You know how rumors are," Silvia said. "Perhaps she ran off with a lover, or perhaps she died in childbirth and it wasn't an entertaining enough story for the gossips. They also say his castle is haunted, but I suppose people are always saying that about very old places."

I turned quickly from the window. Is that truly what they were saying on the street below?

"I'm sure it's only jealousy at your good fortune." Silvia snickered, but then she must have noticed my horrified expression. "Oh dear, Anne, I'm scaring you."

Recovering, I said, "No, I'm quite well. I was surprised, that is all." Were they speculating about why such a wealthy nobleman would need to stoop to peasants to find a bride? I suppose a haunted home was a reasonable enough answer to that question. If one believed in ghosts.

"If a wife fifteen years dead is all we have to worry about, I'm not too concerned," Liesl said. "If nothing else comes of it, we shall have a merry couple of weeks."

I desperately wanted to ask if she meant to accept him if he offered marriage, but I was not sure if she would give me a truthful answer with Silvia present. We chatted a few minutes more, then Liesl made our excuses, and we took our leave.

On our way out, Silvia handed me a basket of books to take on loan, and I thanked her profusely. "This one has ghosts," she said, fondly stroking a red clothbound book. "But don't let that put any ideas into your head about your suitor."

Embarrassed, I mumbled, "Of course not."

It's silly, but I have not been able to stop thinking of the rumors about the runaway wife and the haunted castle. By now, everyone in town must have heard about them, too. I felt their eyes, heavy on us as we left Coesfeld and returned home. Most seemed happy at our good fortune, which would extend to them for the next fortnight at least. A few were perhaps jealous, like Silvia said, but none seemed afraid for us. So why, then, am I?

CHAPTER FIVE

Anne's Diary

16 AUGUST

I have not written since the day after Bluebeard first spoke to our father, when we visited Silvia and Warner in Coesfeld, but oh, how much has happened! Bluebeard has made good on his promise of showing Father and my brothers how well he could take care of Liesl or me.

The last week has been spent with the rest of the village, making merry. During the day, there are hunting and riding parties with the noble friends he has invited, and Bluebeard on his white stallion outshines them all. He also excelled at the swordsmanship display he organized yesterday in the town square. In the evenings, the whole village enjoys feasting and music and dancing with us.

Everyone is happy for my family's good fortune, though I know they continue to gossip about us. It is so sudden and strange—like something from a fairy story. The strangest part, to the villagers at least, is that Bluebeard has not yet declared his intentions on which of us he prefers.

I have overheard whispers at all the lavish events, and if I were vainer, I may no longer call most of the villagers my friends. They all seem to think Liesl, with her long dark hair and charming manner, is the obvious choice.

It is hard not to agree with them. We share a few traits—we're taller than most women, with brown eyes and long, straight noses—but then we diverge. My mousy brown hair is pin-straight, and I have never been as careful of the sun, so my skin is not lily-white like hers. Her figure is lovely and balanced, like the curves of a violin, while mine is wide in the hips and rather too narrow everywhere else. She has also turned down one proposal already, from the butcher's son last year. He was a dull boy, but an eligible match, though no one blamed her for the refusal. Everyone thought her beautiful and good enough to have her pick of any of the village boys. Now she might marry someone from farther beyond our home than the villagers have ever traveled.

Neither Liesl nor I are quite smitten with Bluebeard yet, despite the finery with which he surrounds us. Or at least, though we have not talked of it, it doesn't seem like Liesl is quite ready to say "yes" to him yet. All the expense begins to weigh on me. I rather hope Liesl is the one chosen, for I am still frightened of him.

But this is silly, is it not? He may be older than the knights and princes we dreamt of, but he is at least human. It is not as if I am the princess who must love a frog, or Snow White and Rose Red who must befriend a bear, or any number of young girls from the tales who must grow to love terrifying beasts. Bluebeard is only a man. A man with the power and wealth to make our family secure.

And what must it be like to be the lady of a fine estate like he must own? To ride a fast horse and see so much more of the Westenfall. To never again worry about not having enough milk from the goats for Frau Frida to turn to cheese, or wheat to last through the winter. I could, perhaps, make my secret dream real. Only Liesl, Klaus, and Silvia know of it—that I long to write books. Silvia has assured me that some women do write, sometimes using the names of men. How pleasant it would be to live the life of a noblewoman, with the time and funds to write as many books as I pleased . . .

Our brothers all think him a fine match and have encouraged both of us to accept his offer, should he make one. Heller, who has always cared about gold and wealth more than the rest of us, told us to accept right after Bluebeard first spoke with Father. "It will be a great disservice to the status of our family if neither of you accept him," he said then. "He could set me up as a merchant, and you know what that would mean to me."

The others took a little more persuading, but yesterday even Klaus told us he believes we would be happy if we accept. Gerard declared Bluebeard the finest huntsman he had ever seen and urged us to imagine the stables and wondrous horses they must house. Warner told us to think of the castle library and how many books it must hold, and Ritter reminded us of the paintings and brilliant archi-tecture we'd see—really, that we'd *own*.

Father has been quiet, contemplative, during the festivities. I finally found the courage to approach him today. If it would make him proud for one of us to accept, perhaps that was all the further persuasion I needed.

As the musicians were on a break so they could partake of the feast, there was a lull in the excitement, and I asked Father about his wishes.

"He seems a kind man," he said eventually. "And he can provide for one of you better than I ever could."

His half-smile and the sadness in his eyes made my heart twist. I sat beside him on the bench as the feasting and merriment continued around us. The musicians began to play again, and the townspeople pulled their partners out to dance near the great bonfire in the square. I spotted the butcher's boy sitting at the edge of the fire's glow. Like everyone else, he was pretending not to watch Liesl as she moved among the crowd, though his gaze held more longing and envy than most.

I turned back to my father and placed my hand on his. "I do not wish for grand furnishings and fine horses. I'm happy here. And I think my heart would break if I left home."

We both looked at Liesl, who was now dancing with Bluebeard, a ribbon trailing from each of their hands. A small smile played on her features, but I knew it was not her real one. I thought that my heart would also break for Liesl to marry and leave me behind. But that must happen eventually, and if she could marry a nobleman, become someone important, how could I stop her?

"If that is how you feel, Anne, then let your sister marry him."

Someone passed us with a platter of meat pies, and their aroma, mixed with the smoke of the bonfire, made my mouth water. I nodded slowly. "Have you spoken to her? Does she want this?"

"I have tried. You know your sister—she keeps things close. I believe she could be happy with him. Perhaps you could talk to her tonight."

"Yes," I promised. "I will find out how she feels."

So now I'm tucked up in our bed, waiting for her to come in so I can ask her. She has been acting the part, almost, of the hostess to all of Bluebeard's village events, and she is so natural. Perhaps she really is ready to become his wife and the lady of his castle. I know now that I am not.

Liesl came to bed, smiling and glowing, and said she wanted to tell me a story. She has not told me a bedtime story for a few years, so I think perhaps she meant it as a goodbye, since we will be separated if either of us accept Bluebeard's offer.

Both of us have always loved fairy stories, though for different reasons. She loves voicing the characters, sometimes acting out whole skits for me and our brothers. How she used to make us laugh! I, on the other hand, always loved embellishing the stories, adding my own details or changing the endings.

She chose Bearskin, an old tale.

In it, a young man is approached by a mysterious figure—who our wise young hero discerns to be the devil himself—and is offered riches and good fortune if he will go seven years without bathing or cutting his hair, beard, or nails. He's given a bearskin and a magic coat to wear. He gives his wealth to the poor, asking them to pray that he will live out the full seven years, and many years after, to enjoy his good fortune. After the first year, as you can imagine, he looked rather like a bear himself.

"One day, four years into his curse, he met a weeping man in the woods," Liesl said. "The man wept because he'd lost all his fortune, and his three daughters would starve. Bearskin gave him some of his wealth—he would never be short of it, for the pockets of the coat the devil had given him were always full—and in gratitude, the man offered to allow Bearskin to meet his daughters. He would give one of them to Bearskin as a wife, to thank him for his kindness."

I couldn't imagine our father handing either of us to a stranger so easily, even if he were greatly in that stranger's debt. His reaction to Bluebeard's sudden offer proved he would never do such a thing.

"The daughters, when they met Bearskin, were frightened of him. The eldest two refused to marry him, but the youngest and best sister"—here Liesl nudged me—"felt that he must be a kind man to have helped their father, and that her father's promise must be kept. She agreed to marry Bearskin."

I shivered. Though I knew how the story ended, I still disliked thinking of the poor girl agreeing to marry a man who might as well have been a beast. It was then I began to see why Liesl had chosen this story. Bluebeard may be frightening, but he's neither a bear nor a man who has not bathed in years.

Liesl continued, the familiar cadence of her voice wrapping me in comfort and making my chest ache when I thought of her leaving me. "Bearskin gave the youngest sister half of a ring and kept the other half himself. He promised to return to her in three years, when his curse was lifted. He went through the world, doing good where he could, while the sister stayed behind. She was teased mercilessly about her bridegroom by her other sisters, but she said nothing, resigned to her fate. Every day, she prayed for Bearskin's health.

"At dawn on the seven-year anniversary of his curse, Bearskin went into the woods and again met the devil, who cleaned him up, took back the bearskin, and gave him better clothing. The man was quite handsome now, far more so than he had been before. A life full of good fortune, wealth, and a beautiful wife lay ahead of him."

Liesl began unpinning her hair from its updo and untangling her braids as she spoke. "When he returned to the house of his betrothed, the family did not recognize him. The two eldest sisters tried to charm him, but he ignored them and pulled the youngest sister into his arms. After showing his half of the ring, he declared himself to be her betrothed and kissed her. She wept with happiness, and they were married that day."

When I was young, I couldn't bear to hear the last part of the story and needed it to end with the young couple's happiness. I wondered if Liesl would omit it, since this story seemed her parting gift to me. But she took a deep breath and continued.

"The sisters, upon hearing that the handsome young man was Bearskin, and that he and his wealth and good fortune could have been theirs, flew into a rage. One hanged herself from a tree, and the other threw herself into a well and drowned. The next day, the devil called upon the young man once more. 'You see,' he said, grinning with wickedness. 'Now I have two souls for the one of yours.'"

Those words, spoken in Liesl's voice in the darkness dozens of times before, should not affect me anymore, but a great chill ran through me.

Liesl took my hands in hers then. "Anne," she said. "I am thinking of accepting Bluebeard. But I cannot do to you what Bearskin's bride did to her sisters." She shuddered and closed her eyes.

"Is this what has worried you, Liesl? I do not care for him as you do. Worry not." I tried to keep the relief from my voice.

She let go of my hands and looked toward the ladder to our loft, as if to be sure our father and brothers still slept below. "You will think me terrible, but I do not care for him either. Not in that way."

"I could never think you terrible." Her posture relaxed, but she still would not look at me, so I asked quietly, "But if you do not feel anything for him, why are you going to accept?"

She sighed as if I'd said something rather childish. "How many other suitors are lining up for my hand? This is the wealthiest man we are ever likely to meet. And he is taken with us."

"But if you don't love him—"

Liesl finally met my gaze then, and there was steel in her eyes that I had never seen before. "I will learn to love him. Like the bride in the story. There are many stories like that, are there not?" she asked. "Even if I do not, our family will be taken care of for the rest of our lives. That is enough for me."

My stomach turned at the thought of Liesl being taken from me, swept off to his castle to live out her days in lonely comfort. My voice was small and unsure when I said, "But we'll be apart."

She smiled then. It was the first genuine one I'd seen her wear today. The others were for show, but this one was real. For me. "That is the best part. We don't have to be. I've spoken to Bluebeard today, and he has agreed that, when I marry him, you will come to live with us."

At first, I was delighted. I thought of the sumptuous dinners, the gowns I would wear, dancing to sweeping music at glorious balls. To have a garden in which to stroll—one whose purpose is beauty for the eyes and not food for the belly. It was as if we were living in one of our favorite tales, and Bluebeard would make all our dreams come true, just as the prince did for Cinderella.

"You will come, will you not?" The dreamy look on my face made her smile, and she threw her arms around me when I nodded my assent.

I was grateful she couldn't see my face as we embraced, because it was then I began to doubt. Even now, I worry. Bluebeard is no ordinary man, and not just because of his castle and riches. The others in the village sense it too. He pulls everyone's eyes, but no one draws too near, as if afraid to be in his shadow. And what of the rumors of his haunted castle? The tales of his wife, run away into the night, who perhaps met with some terrible fate?

Is Liesl as frightened of him as I am? Or is she strong enough to withstand it? Perhaps she is like Bearskin's bride—able to see what others cannot. If she is brave, I can be, too.

"Yes," I said as I hugged her tighter. "You will be a beautiful bride. I'm so glad I won't have to be without you."

She pulled away. "It's settled then. I'll tell Father." She climbed down the ladder to the first floor, where our father and three of our brothers slept.

When she left, I pulled out my journal so I could write this. I now feel both fear and excitement for what awaits us at Bluebeard's castle. I'll be able to fill these pages with everything new and wonderful we'll see, but there is also some guilt that Liesl is so much braver than I. Perhaps it will appease my conscience if I vow to do everything I can to make her happy and keep us both safe in a strange new place.

It is an easy vow to make, after all.

CHAPTER SIX

Letter from Liesl

19 AUGUST

D earest Mother,

It has been some time since I last wrote to you, but I think of you every single day. The letters have become scarcer over the years—not because I need you any less, but, I suppose, because I have learned better how to live without you.

My promise to look after the family when you no longer could weighs heavily on me, and I do my best to fulfill it every day.

And oh, Mama, I'm so happy to tell you that my time has come—I've finally found a way to make sure the whole family, but especially Anne and Klaus, of whom I am always most protective, will be taken care of for the rest of our lives. It came from such an unexpected quarter, it is like something out of the tales of magic Anne loves so much.

A nobleman—a very wealthy one, if the rumors are to be believed, or if one tallies up the cost of his efforts in wooing me—has asked for my hand in marriage. I have accepted, though, of course, I made sure it would not break Anne's heart to do so first. In fact, she will be joining me at the castle, because it would break *my* heart to leave her.

Bluebeard—that is the nickname the lord goes by—seemed as if he would be quite happy with either of us as a wife. It might bother me if he was someone I had fallen in love with, but it certainly does not matter the way things are. He has been kind to me, generous to my family, and though it is strange, I will not question whatever reasons he has to take a peasant for a wife.

I think perhaps the last time I wrote was when I turned down my first offer of marriage from the butcher's boy. I was not sure, then, if I was right to refuse him. I could have made a happy enough life with him in the village, I suppose, even if I didn't love him like you did Father.

But now I know that I was right to wait—that I'm destined for more. To think I shall be lady of a castle, managing an entire estate. Someone important.

I am to be wed in a few days. As the momentous day draws near, I find that the thought of a wedding without you makes me melancholy and listless. But you will be there, will you not? I like to fancy that you check in with us now and then, from your peace in the afterlife. This turn of events has been such a stroke of fortune that I almost fancy you may have had a hand in it. Perhaps you are helping us in mysterious ways, from beyond the grave.

I miss you more than words can say.

With all my love,

Your daughter, Liesl

CHAPTER SEVEN

Anne's Diary

26 AUGUST

It could not have been a more beautiful day for a wedding.

My messy handwriting shall have to be excused—Liesl and I are bumping along in Bluebeard's carriage, and it is a wonder I can write at all, or that I have not overturned the ink bottle with all this rattling.

But yes—it was a perfect day for a wedding. The sky blue and clear, a faint breeze keeping the heat at bay and spreading the scent of honeysuckle. My sister looked glorious.

Bluebeard had wanted to order her a decadent dress of lace sewn with pearls, but it would have taken so long to send for dressmakers of that skill that he decided against it. Liesl said she was relieved anyway. She always wanted to be married in a simple, gauzy white gown adorned only with flowers, and so she was. Though instead of wildflowers from the meadow, she carried a bouquet and wore a crown of pink and blood-red roses. They were striking against her shining dark hair and brought out the blush of her cheeks.

I wore a simpler crown of moth mullein blooms and a dress that matched their white petals and pink centers. It was certainly the finest thing I had ever worn. The villagers celebrated as my family made our way to the church, where Bluebeard waited for his bride. Our village is always festive for weddings, but as all the townspeople had been renewed by Bluebeard's purse during Liesl's courtship, hers was the most splendid I have ever seen. Flowers adorned every surface, and the villagers called out well-wishes to Liesl, waving streamers from their upper windows as we proceeded through the twisting streets. Others played instruments—fiddles and tin-whistles, flutes and drums—singing and dancing with abandon all the way to the chapel.

The wedding proceeded as I suppose all weddings do—the priest solemn and stately, the vows made, rings exchanged, and not a dry eye in the whole church.

Bluebeard threw yet another feast for the villagers, with dancing and laughter and fast-flowing wine. We made merry all evening and into the wee hours of the morning. Liesl seemed so happy that my heart ached for our good fortune, though I secretly yearned for my own turn. Someday, I hope, someone will want to entwine his life with mine the way Bluebeard did Liesl's. Though, of course, I would prefer if he were a bit closer to my own age, and perhaps not so wealthy or intimidating.

Only once during all the festivities did anything temper my joy. Klaus pulled me aside during a break from his fiddle-playing. His serious expression worried me, and I followed him to a spot just outside the glow of the bonfire, where no one else should hear us.

"Anne," Klaus said. "Oh Annie, tomorrow you leave me, and what shall I do then?" He half-smiled and tousled my hair. I wriggled out of his grasp before he could do any lasting damage to the flower crown or my braids.

"You shall be quite happy to be rid of me, I should think, but for my help with the milking."

"It is true," he said. "The goats do not behave so well for any of us. They like your gentle nature."

I smiled to myself and found my eyes suddenly stinging. I would miss him greatly, but I must not begin to cry or I would not be able to stop.

His smile faded, and Klaus took a step closer, glancing around to be sure no one paid us any mind. "Your gentle nature is also what worries me."

"What do you mean?"

He sighed, wiped a hand down his face, then met my eyes again. "There are whispers," he said. "I don't know what to think, but people have been saying things about Bluebeard . . ."

I waited, my fears surfacing again. Had Klaus heard something more about his last wife or the haunted castle? We'd discussed the ghosts before and laughed, but he was grim-faced now. All along, I'd thought us too fortunate, that Bluebeard sweeping us off to his estate was something from a dream. Perhaps these whispers were the chink in the armor, the missing piece that would make it all fit together.

Klaus exhaled again, looking at the bonfire instead of at me. He wished not to tell me this, not to spoil Liesl's marriage or my adventure. But he did tell me, because he's a good brother. The best I have.

"They say . . . they say that he has been married before. Several times. And that no one knows what happened to his wives."

"*Wives?*" I asked. Had there been others before the one who had run away? "How many?"

Klaus shook his head. "I don't know. You know how rumors go. I hear reports of anywhere from three to seven. But I believe there is some truth there, underneath all of the embellishments."

I clasped my hands together to stop them from shaking and nodded solemnly. "Thank you for telling me, Klaus," I said when I was finally able to untie my tongue.

"I couldn't bring myself to tell Liesl, lest I spoil her day, but I wanted to caution you. I hope the rumors are untrue," he said. "Perhaps it was only the one wife, as he said. Or if there were others, perhaps they just grew tired of that strange beard of his and ran off."

"It is possible," I said. My voice came out flat and empty. *One* wife may have run, as the rumors said, but three? *Seven?*

Klaus squeezed my hand. "Promise you shall write to me. I'll worry for you and Liesl."

"I swear it." I smiled, but my heart felt heavy. I was sure to gain so much by going, but how much was I also leaving behind? What would I do without Father and Silvia and dear Klaus?

Bluebeard rode for his castle once the festivities died down, saying he had business there and must ensure his staff readied it for his new bride before her arrival. Liesl and I slept one last time in our bed in the loft, and at the break of dawn the next morning, we said our goodbyes.

Klaus nobly withheld his tears, and Ritter gave me a sketch of our family that I shall treasure always. For Liesl, he'd painted a small portrait of her and Bluebeard in their wedding finery. Silvia and Warner hugged us tightly and gave me a lovely little book of fairy stories that I'd borrowed from them at least a dozen times. Gerard and Heller had little to say, but they were solemn, for once setting aside their boisterous jokes. I think even they felt how much this would change our family.

Father was the hardest, though. His eyes shone with tears, and I could see the effort it took him to smile. "My girls," he said as he clasped each of our hands in his work-roughened ones. "I never thought I'd see you off to a new home so far from me." It took him a moment to collect himself, but then he said, "We are all so blessed by Liesl's marriage. I wish you both all the happiness in the world. You must write to us of everything wonderful you're sure to experience at the castle."

My own tears were falling freely by then. With all our daydreams of fairy stories and far-flung adventures, I'd never expected it would be so difficult when it came time to leave. To say goodbye to all we'd known.

When Father crushed me into one last embrace, he whispered that he loved me and asked me to take care of Liesl. I assured him I would, and I am sure she promised to look out for me as well.

And now I really must stop writing of home or the mist in my eyes will become a flood. I shall see them again, of course. It is not a forever parting.

We have been journeying in the carriage for several days, sleeping and changing horses at inns along the way. I have been too jangled about and stomach-ill to write until today, but it seems that finally I have become used to the roads. Of course, I should not become accustomed to it until today, when our journey is nearly finished and we shall reach the castle sometime after nightfall.

The landscape has changed as we traveled, from familiar meadows and fields skirted by far-off mountains to dense forests and views of much taller, snow-capped mountains. Towns nestle along the rivers cutting through the valleys, and crumbling castles sit perched high on peaks. Strange to think I should live in one soon.

Liesl is asleep across from me now. I suppose she is tired from the celebrations of the last few weeks. The curtains are a little open so that light spills across her face and illuminates the dark, inky sapphire of her wedding ring. She looks the way I always imagined the princesses in our stories to look, and rightly so, for with what else can we compare our good fortune? But could she also be in danger?

Earlier today, I tried to tell her what Klaus had told me, the rumors about Bluebeard's many wives. She became cross, told me I'm old enough to know better than to pay heed to gossip, and that I should be grateful, thanking God for our good fortune. She is right, I suppose.

I feel guilt and relief in equal measure that it is Liesl he has married instead of me. And now that I shall live in the castle with her, I feel even more guilt that I should have much of the reward without doing anything to merit it. She is like Bearskin's bride or the princess who kissed a frog and turned him back into a prince. I am too cautious and cowardly to earn what those heroines did. But Liesl is brave.

I think back to our dreams in the meadow. How could we know that such a nobleman on a white steed would come? I suppose it is proof we do not dream that the man who did come and sweep us away has a ghastly blue beard and is followed by whispers of missing past wives.

All my life, I've had Father and five older brothers and Liesl watching out for me. I have never needed to protect anyone—not even myself. Now, I must protect Liesl. She has done so much for our family by marrying Bluebeard. I am still unsure if she truly feels any affection for him, or what other dreams she may have surrendered to follow this path. For my part, I will do anything I can to keep us both safe and happy as we enter this new world.

CHAPTER EIGHT

Letter from Anne

1 SEPTEMBER

Dearest Klaus,

By now you should have received the short letter I scrawled off to let you know of our safe arrival at Bluebeard's home. I am glad you and our dear father and brothers were able to attend the wedding vows in our chapel back home and the merriment that followed, but oh, how I miss you now. Perhaps you are missing us, too. I wanted to take this moment to send you a more detailed account of our first days here.

There is much to learn, more than I would have expected. Though I'm far from a natural, the riding lessons have been my favorite—how jealous Gerard will be if he ever sees these horses himself! If only riding were the only thing we need to know.

Our village prepared us with some of the basic dances, but there are many formal ones that we must know. There has also been a great deal more about table settings and other silly bits of etiquette than I had thought possible. I do not mind learning new things, but it is difficult to remember them when my questions about the reasons behind these traditions are always met with the housekeeper's "That is the way things are done, Fraulein."

She is a rather fearsome creature, Idonia. Though she is older than Frau Frida, her spine is pin-straight and her dark hair, which is always pulled into a tight bun, has only one streak of white. The servants skitter out of her way when she walks into a room, lest they be berated by the flood of criticisms she has ready at any moment. She frightens me, a little. Idonia is the only person I have never seen smile.

I should not complain of our lessons when we live in such luxury. We have lived in Tiefenwald Castle for several days now and have still not managed to explore all the rooms! A great many are locked up except for when he hosts guests, but even then, there are many unlocked ones we have not managed to see. Of course, Liesl was so overwhelmed the first day, meeting the servants and settling into her role of mistress of the house, that we did not have much time to venture beyond our quarters except for meals, which are served at the long dining table in the Great Hall. It has been no difficulty, as my room is beautiful and nearly as large as our home—imagine it, when eight people used to share our small cottage! I have two lovely windows overlooking the forest and a great canopied bed.

Once over the initial shock, we were able to explore other rooms—the ballroom with its crystal chandeliers laden with candles and panels of oil paintings on every wall, a lovely sitting room just like the inside of a jewelry box, and the great marble staircase leading from the main entrance to the second floor. Parts of the castle are old, fraught with creaks and drafts, but the portions in which we spend our time are so lovely that we hardly notice them. We've seen so much beauty that I could fill several more pages describing it all, but since I am sure there is much more in store for us, and since I do not wish to bore you with too many details, I shall merely tell you of my two favorite rooms.

The first to capture my heart was the conservatory. I do so love flowers and plants, and to have such beautiful greenery indoors made me smile with delight. Green is the best color, is it not? And to think we shall have it all the year, even in midwinter! The floor is a mosaic of tiles in greens and blues. The walls are entirely made of glass to let in the sunlight, and it is always warmer than the rest of the castle—none of those frequent icy drafts find their way here. The ceiling, too, is made of glass, so that if I tiptoe down there at night while the rest of the castle sleeps, I can make out a slice of moon and a few faint stars through the leaves. I do not yet know who tends the plants there or the lovely gardens surrounding the castle, but I must find out soon as I should dearly like to help and learn from them.

I have also fallen deeply in love with one other room: Bluebeard's library. Liesl and I have taken to spending our mornings there, nestled together on the overstuffed sofas piled with pillows and cushions. Liesl works on her lacework or embroidery while I pore over novels. Except for two broad stained-glass windows which spill red, yellow, and green light across the Oriental rugs, the entire walls are covered in bookshelves. They go up to the ceiling, so that a ladder is required to reach the upper shelves. How I wish I could show Warner and Silvia! Seeing so many books in one place does something to my soul, and I do not feel such peace anywhere else here. It is as far removed from our little cottage as a place may be, but somehow it feels like home.

Speaking of home, how I dearly miss you all! I know it has been but a few days, but still, it is longer than we have ever spent apart before. How is Sophie, my little gray goat? I was particularly fond of her. Has Gerard recovered from the loss of his new favorite hunting partner?

Do tell Father and the others how we are: happy and well. I must go now, for Liesl calls me. Tonight is our first ball, so I'm sure tomorrow I shall have even more to tell you! Please write soon, even if my second letter does not arrive with this one. Your words shall help ease my homesickness, which I feel keenly, despite all the glamour of my new home.

With all my love, your sister,

Anne

CHAPTER NINE

Anne's Diary

1 SEPTEMBER

I have just finished writing to Klaus, and though my fingers grow rather ink-stained, there is one thing more of which I wish to write. An incident this morning has rather unsettled me. I did not wish to worry anyone, so I said nothing to Liesl and did not mention it in my letter to Klaus, but I still feel I must express it somehow. So I shall write.

After breakfast today, I took to wandering the castle halls. Liesl was meeting with the staff about tonight's ball and declined my help when I offered it. I would rather have wandered the gardens and grounds—alone except for the slim, dark-haired figure I see on occasion, who I suspect is the gardener—but it rained and thundered all day, so I contented myself with exploring inside.

The Grand Gallery is a beautiful room. The walls are papered in pink-and-red satin stripes and hung with oil paintings in intricate gilt frames. I could spend many an hour in that room, examining paintings of Bluebeard's ancestors and pastoral scenes that make me long for home, and I spent an hour or two doing so this morning. How Ritter would love to see that room! It has been under a week, and I already miss my family and am hoping they can visit. Perhaps at Christmas they can come to us, and I'll show this room to Ritter and the rest of them.

As I stepped closer to a portrait of a pale, white-haired woman with a dachshund placed among her voluminous skirts, something ran by out in the hall. I thought it might be a dog or a cat, but found it strange since I had never seen Bluebeard's hunting dogs within the castle. I stepped out into the hall but only caught a glimpse of a white-tipped tail as the creature turned the corner.

Picking up my skirts so I would not trip over them, I ran after the animal. This time it stopped at the entrance to one of the spiral stairs that wound through the castle's towers. The towers nearer the castle entrance were kept in better repair, but this was one of the larger, crumbling stone towers.

I saw then that it was not one of the hunting dogs or even a cat, but a red fox. The sight of it, looking back at me with its amber eyes as if to make sure I was still following, surprised me so much that I nearly tripped and fell in the hall. How had it entered the castle? Bluebeard loved to hunt foxes—a live one was not safe here.

But I did not have much time to contemplate this before the fox turned and ran down the steps. I still had the strange sense that it wanted me to follow, and I also hoped I could help it get back outside where it might be safe, so I hurried after it.

That tower of the castle must not see much use, for the sconces were not lit, and the air was rather stale. The only light spilled through in shafts from the arrow slits in the castle wall, barely enough to see the flashes of red fur ahead of me. I reached where I thought a door should be to the main level of the castle, and then the lower level, but the steps kept winding down, the curved walls doorless. The air grew chill as I descended, and goosebumps rose on my arms.

The stairs finally led to a dirt-packed floor, so unlike the other halls of the castle, which all had mosaics or checkerboard tiles or fine wooden flooring. Scant light streamed down through the stairwell, and I wished I had thought to take a candle with me. It was too late to go back for one then, or I would lose the fox.

As I peered into the gloom and let my eyes adjust, the fox sat down outside a door midway along the stone-walled corridor. The air here, an unknown distance below the main castle, was somehow both cold and stifling in its mustiness. A deep sense of foreboding came over me, and I stepped further into the darkness slowly.

What was I doing, following a woodland creature into the depths of the castle? I got only far enough to make out that the door was made of heavy wood with broad iron hinges, and had words carved into a wooden plaque in its middle, when a sharp voice from behind made me jump.

"What are you doing down here?"

I spun around to see a woman silhouetted in the meager light from the stairwell. I recognized her voice; it was Idonia. She must know the castle better than the other servants, having been here longest. Though she is old enough to be my grandmother, her high cheekbones betray the severe beauty she must have had when she was younger.

It was not clear what I had done wrong, but I felt guilty under her gaze anyway.

"I . . . there was a fox—" But when I turned and pointed, the fox had vanished. Perhaps it was never there at all, only an illusion brought on by homesickness or exhaustion from our travels or being overwhelmed by everything new here. I shook my head. "It's gone now. I'm sorry," I added, though I still was not quite sure what I was apologizing for.

"All is well," Idonia said as I approached. Her face was still shadowed so I couldn't see her expression. "But you must not come down here again, Fraulein. It is not kept up, and you might hurt yourself, and we should not find you for days."

I did not believe that, as I had only been down there a few minutes, and she had managed to find me. But I was still cowed by her words and felt so guilty that I merely nodded and meekly followed her back up the steps, with one last glance to be sure the fox was not there. Perhaps it never had been.

Now I am not sure what to think of the incident. I was so sure I'd seen the fox, and I have not been one to imagine such things since I was quite a little girl. Idonia had seemed angry and frightened, and I do not think what I did justified either emotion. Why should she care if I wandered about in the halls beneath the castle? Is it not my home now as well? I can think of no reason, besides the supposed safety concerns she gave, but it makes me wary of her.

Rereading what I've written of the incident, I feel silly about the whole affair. Everyone else here has been so kind and welcoming—all the servants dote on Liesl, and she seems happy. I've seen little of Bluebeard, but he has planned splendid balls in her honor. Everyone has made us feel so at home, even in this vast castle, that I must brush off this one incident with Idonia and move forward. There is the ball this evening, the first I have ever attended, and I must let the servants begin readying my dress and hair. It is so different from our village dances, where Liesl and I would braid each other's hair and wear our flower crowns. Tonight, I shall wear a new gown edged in lace, and my maidservant Cristina will curl my hair and weave it with pearls.

There is much to do, so I shall not dwell on the fox any further. Still, I should very much like to know what is in that room where it led me.

Oh, how happy and light I feel! It is so very late—the sun shall rise soon—but I wanted to capture this feeling before I fall asleep. Liesl and I looked splendid in our finery, and we danced and ate and drank the night away under the crystal chandeliers of the ballroom. The music played by the orchestra was soaring and melodious, and at one point in the night, as I glimpsed Liesl smiling and laughing as my partner spun me in a waltz, I wanted to cry with happiness.

My feet ache, but I do not mind at all. We are just like the twelve princesses in the tale, who danced the night away and wore out their shoes.

How is it that only a few weeks ago, the greatest adventure we had known was searching for a runaway goat? I feel as if all our dreams, the ones we had talked of so often in our meadow, have come true.

Chapter Ten

Bluebeard's Diary | Cacilie

23 June, 14th Year of King Lukas II

My experiments have been fruitless. I've just sent away the alchemist who has lived beneath my castle these last two years. His ideas, in the end, yielded nothing but damage to my treasury. But it is no matter now. I believe I have found another way.

I've always been interested in alchemy. Though my coffers are full and my land is so fertile that I have little need to turn iron to gold, eternal life is another matter. A few years ago, there was an accident. While out hunting, my stallion lost his footing in a fast-flowing river, and I found myself dragged under. I reemerged a quarter-league downstream and clawed my way to shore, half-drowned. As I coughed up water on the banks, a truth I'd perhaps always known crystallized for me: I must not die. I am meant for far more than that.

Cacilie does not understand my quest for immortality. "We are blessed, my darling. Why spend your days searching for ways to extend your life when you could enjoy the time we have now?" Sometimes, she blushes and adds, "We could try again for an heir—that is how most men extend their legacies, is it not?"

These conversations only show how little she knows me. I have no desire for an heir, and I am most certainly unlike "most men." Perhaps unlike any other man alive. Why should I, who have greatly grown my wealth and influence over my forty brief years, not live eighty, one hundred, two hundred more to enjoy them? To give everything to an unworthy heir who has not worked as I have . . . I can only hold such a thought with disdain.

I thought I loved her once, that with her voluptuous beauty and quick mind, she would be almost an equal to me. Perhaps I was wrong.

At least I know how I shall find out. After all my years of searching, I have found a way to fulfill my fate, to extend my life indefinitely. From the most unexpected source, too.

Tonight, I shall share what I have learned with my wife. If Cacilie sees the value in it, if she sees why the price must be paid and agrees to take her place by my side, as something closer to God than man, I will know she is truly meant to be my partner after all.

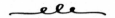

Alas, Cacilie does not see the matter as I do.

She was horrified. In tears, she said the idea was of the devil and that she felt she did not know me anymore. The sentiment was mutual, then. She would not agree to try the spell, even when I ordered her as her husband and lord. Ah, well. It saves me the trouble of searching for a person who will not be missed.

Tonight, in the very room my alchemist occupied this morning, I shall attempt the ritual.

CHAPTER ELEVEN

Letter from Anne

4 SEPTEMBER

Dearest Klaus,

The first ball and the dinner before it were everything I had hoped they would be! In fact, there has been so much excitement that it is now several days after I intended to write, and we have had plenty of dinners and balls to celebrate Bluebeard and Liesl's wedding with all his noble friends. I do not think he has spared any expense—indeed, I do not think he frets over any cost, whether for the balls or for our own comfort. Liesl and I have our every need supplied, sometimes before we ask. The servants are all so kind and attentive—I'm especially fond of the cook—though it is still such a strange thing to have servants.

I would like to give you the full details of the revelry, but I can imagine your eyes beginning to droop at the tiresome details. I will try to be brief in my accounts. Liesl is an absolute jewel. Everyone loves her here, and she always looks so beautiful. At the first ball, she wore a gown of pale pink, and she looked like a delicate rose petal. Her dress for the second ball was peach, with an intricate lace bodice. The third night she wore a gauzy gown in a soft yellow, like candlelight. I cannot imagine what she shall wear tonight, though I have teased her that she is attempting to wear the entire rainbow!

The house is abuzz with guests from all over the kingdom and beyond, and there are many lavish wedding gifts. Bluebeard is so used to this life that he takes little joy in them, but Liesl and I certainly do. Everything here is opulent, and we are bathed in luxury, surrounded by only the finest silks, the softest velvet, sparkling jewels, and delightfully delicate chocolates. Bluebeard arranged for a string quartet to delight us with a private concert one evening, which was a nice change from the nightly balls. How I wish you could be here to hear the glorious music! Perhaps someday you could become a concert violinist like the ones who play for us.

There are even some fine young knights and nobles who have begun to court me. I can have a partner for every dance if I wish, and indeed last night I grew weary of such attentions. I left early and spent a relaxing evening perusing books in the library.

I am now inclined to believe that Bluebeard is not such a strange man after all.

Your letter brought joy to Liesl and me, and I hope you shall write often. I'm glad that Bluebeard was prompt in fulfilling his promise to send the family a stipend and set Heller up as a merchant. Perhaps

Heller will not be quite so surly now that he has what he has always wanted.

I hope all else is well at home. Pass along our love to Father, Warner, Silvia, Gerard, Heller, and Ritter. I miss you dearly, Klaus. I hope you will be able to visit soon and see this fine castle, though I know the journey is a long and costly one.

Yours truly,

Anne

CHAPTER TWELVE

Anne's Diary

5 SEPTEMBER

There are moments when I am quite content and happy here—snuggled up with one of the library's many books, strolling the lovely gardens, or dancing in the arms of dashing young noblemen. But other times, living here is harder than I ever expected it to be.

Last night, the ball began later than usual, so Bluebeard, Liesl, and I had a private dinner. It was strange to sit at the long table and see most of it empty. And to be so near Bluebeard. Generally, I am seated rather far down the table so he can give better status to his most loyal friends. In fact, I have hardly seen Bluebeard since arriving. He spends much of his time hunting—the bear and boar and stag heads hanging in the Great Hall are a testament to his prowess. I have, occasionally, seen him about the castle, checking his reflection in its many mirrors to ensure his waist-length beard is in order.

He said little at dinner, mostly making satisfied grunts at the meal. I found it a bit ungentlemanlike, but then again, what do I know of gentlemen?

Liesl, however, was also withdrawn. I tried several subjects to no avail. She seemed determined to focus on moving tiny bites of food to her mouth, chewing, and swallowing. Perhaps she had too much on her mind with all the events we have been hosting.

"Tonight's ball will be lovely," I said, trying once more to ignite a conversation. "It was a clear day. It will be a perfect night for dancing under the stars."

"Yes, I believe it will be," Liesl said.

The ball of conversation—as Idonia liked to call it in our lessons—fell unwanted on the table between us once again. I had to hold in a sigh of frustration. However, as the servants removed our entrees and began distributing our desserts, I rallied again.

"Would you like to walk in the gardens with me tomorrow?" I asked Liesl. "You haven't been out with me in days. The exercise might do you good."

"I am perfectly well," Liesl said with a glance at Bluebeard, but he paid us no mind as he dug into his marbled cake. "And in any case, I shall have plenty of fresh air at the ball tonight."

"How about a ride, then? We must improve if we want to ride along the next time we host a hunt."

Liesl sighed. "I really have a great deal to do. Tomorrow's ball is an important one. We are hosting the ambassador from Rheinsburg."

"Oh." I was not even sure where Rheinsburg was, so little had I ever heard it mentioned. "Well, perhaps I could help you." I'd offered a few times before, and she'd always declined, so I did not expect it when she agreed this time.

"I suppose that would be alright," she said. "Meet me here tomorrow at ten, and you can help me choose the place settings and flower arrangements."

Something felt off, still. There seems to be a bit of a rift between Liesl and me as of late, and I cannot understand it. She is so pleasant-yet-authoritative with the servants, so friendly and open with all the upper-class strangers who attend her events. So why is she so distant from me, her closest companion for so many years?

But I did not question it, instead ensuring that I arrived in the dining hall a few minutes before ten this morning. I was tired from the dancing that went into the wee hours of the morning, but opportunities to spend time with my sister were so few and far between now that I knew I had to take this one.

"Yes, this will do very well, Idonia." Liesl was saying as I entered. "Thank you."

Idonia motioned to some of the other servants, and they began clearing the half-dozen different table settings and flower arrangements that had been laid out.

"Good morning, Liesl," I said. "Idonia."

"Morning." My sister didn't even look at me; she just ran a line through a couple of items from her list.

"You already decided on the table settings?" I asked, trying not to sound disappointed. "What's next? Maybe I can help—"

"Idonia," Liesl interrupted. "You're excused. Please have the servants retire as well. Meet me in the ballroom in a quarter of an hour, and we will discuss other arrangements for tonight."

"Very well, Mistress," Idonia said, curtsying and sweeping out of the room.

"Liesl, what's the matter?"

"Nothing is the matter," she said. "Everything will be perfect tonight."

I ran my finger along the beveled edge of the table. "What can I help with?"

She stared at her list, but I could tell she wasn't reading it. "Nothing," she finally said.

I bit my lip. "Did I do something wrong? I don't understa—"

"Of course you don't," Liesl snapped. "You're still just a girl."

My face heated, though I wasn't sure if it was more from anger or embarrassment. "So?" I asked. "It's not as if I need to be married to choose *table settings*."

"Leave me, Anne. I have much to do." Her voice was sharp, much sharper than any other time she'd scolded me.

I would have insisted again, but it was clear she did not want my help. So instead, I turned on my heel and half-ran to my chambers, hoping no one would see the angry tears I was failing to hold back.

Cristina was in my room, making the bed. I swiped at my eyes, managing to control my expression enough to smile at her. Then I had what I thought was an excellent idea.

"Hello, Cristina," I said. "How are you?"

"Good morning, Fraulein," she said, her smile rounding her cheeks. "I am well, and yourself?"

I didn't much want to answer that question, so instead, I got to my point. "Would you like to take a turn about the garden with me? I thought we could cut some flowers for my room." Her eyes moved to the side, and an almost-grimace passed over her face. "I mean—for your room too, if you want, of course," I added.

"I'm sorry, Fraulein, but that wouldn't be proper." She finished making the bed, running a hand over the brocade to smooth out the wrinkles.

"Oh, well, if you don't want flowers, then we could just—"

"Fraulein Anne," Cristina said softly. "I'm sure you will make friends among the young ladies of your own class soon enough, as you become used to your new life here. As for me, well, Idonia would have my hide if I were to go frolicking in the gardens with you instead of doing my duties here."

"Oh," I said, my face burning for the second time today. "Of course. I'm sorry, Cristina, I didn't think—"

"It was very kind of you to ask," she said. "Good day, Fraulein." Then she curtsied and left, taking my old linens with her.

I shut the door behind her and leaned against it, then sank down to a seat on the floor. I stayed there for a long time, too ashamed to face anyone. Cristina had so easily seen everything that I had felt but not yet put into words. That I was lonely. That I didn't belong here, at least not yet. That I probably never would.

Perhaps Liesl, who has stepped into her role as if she had trained for it her whole life, can see it too, and that's why she has no patience for me. For the one who can't quite keep up.

Curse it. I've let a tear fall and smudge the ink.

I must work harder to belong here. To deserve to be here. I think I shall start with improving my riding. The goats always liked me so well and did as I bade them—perhaps horses will, too. Tomorrow I'll take out my favorite horse, and I won't come back until I seem as if I were born astride it.

Chapter Thirteen

Anne's Diary

6 September

I met a boy today. Well, I have been meeting many boys of late, at the balls and dinner parties, but this one is different. I went out for a ride on the dappled gray gelding, just as I had planned, and came across a little house at the edge of the forest, near a copse of birches. I'd thought all the servants lived within the castle walls, but I was incorrect. The gardener does not.

His name is Sebastian, and it is he who manages Bluebeard's gardens, as well as the beautiful plants in the conservatory. I had often wondered who to thank for the splendid roses and colorful lilies, and had glimpsed him a few times, but I had never expected the gardener responsible for all this to be quite so young. My age, I think.

He is tall and thin, his skin paler than I would have expected for someone who spends so much time outdoors, although it could have been from the contrast of his ink-black hair. His nose is crooked and his chin a bit too pointed, but to use the word "handsome" would not be an exaggeration. So, of course, I was clumsy and awkward and utterly bungled our first conversation.

"Sebastian," I said from atop my horse after he'd introduced himself. "Nice to meet you. I'm Anne. You probably already know my sister."

"Yes," he said, leaning on the rake he'd been using. "I've helped with the flowers at all the balls and such."

"They're very nice," I said. "I had some questions about the beds to the south of the castle." My horse was getting impatient, snorting and shifting from foot to foot, and he turned so I was facing away from Sebastian. I wasn't ready to leave, but the horse apparently wasn't ready to listen to me.

"Do you need help?" Sebastian asked as I pulled on the reins, trying to get the beast to turn back around.

"No, no," I said, mentally kicking myself. The horse wouldn't budge, which meant I should dismount, something I'd only done a few times unassisted. And those few times had not been graceful. I kicked my feet out of the stirrups and meant to slide off as smoothly as my sidesaddle would allow, but then the horse moved again, and I found myself clinging to the saddle to stay on, my legs dangling.

"Whoa there," Sebastian said, dropping his rake in the dirt. He calmed the horse and then grabbed my waist, gently guiding me until my feet hit solid ground.

"Thank you," I said, utterly embarrassed as I pulled away from him. The places on my sides his where hands had touched felt nearly as hot as my face. Silk dresses are rather thin, after all.

"He doesn't trust you." The gardener had taken the reins and was running a hand over the gelding's flanks. The traitorous horse was now docile and accommodating.

"Well, the feeling is mutual," I said, pushing the hair that had freed itself from my braid behind my ears.

"That's the problem."

I crossed my arms, now remembering my conversation with Cristina. I wasn't supposed to be having friendly chats with servants. I needed to be more like Liesl. "What would you know about horses?" I asked. "You just said you're the gardener."

"I help out in the stables in the winter, and whenever they need extra hands."

"Oh."

Sebastian rubbed a spot behind the horse's ears, which seemed to make him happy, as he nickered. Not for the first time, I wished we'd had horses to ride growing up instead of just our old plow horse. I was so terrified of falling from one.

"How do you like your new home, Fraulein?"

"It's Anne," I said before I remembered that I was trying to be like Liesl. He only smiled and waited for my answer. "It's lovely," I finally said, but it came out flat.

"Is it?" he asked, arching an eyebrow.

"Of course," I said. "As I'm sure you've heard, we don't come from this world."

"I had heard something like that," he said. Then he grinned. "And even if I hadn't, I could tell by your riding."

My mouth fell open, but I couldn't think of a clever retort.

"I don't mean to offend, Fraulein Anne," he said. Then he led the horse closer to me. "Would you like a riding lesson?"

"I've had riding lessons," I said.

"Not with me."

I couldn't deny that, and after remembering my failure with Liesl yesterday, I allowed him to help me up onto the horse again. But then he stuck one foot into the lower stirrup and swung his other leg up behind me, somehow unhindered by the lack of a stirrup on the other side of this wretched lady's saddle.

"You're riding with me?" I asked. This didn't seem at all appropriate.

"Yes," he said. Then, perhaps as he also realized this was unconventional, he added, "The horse trusts me."

That froze any argument on my tongue. He kicked the horse into motion, gently guiding my hands on the reins. We traveled along a broad path through the woods that followed a river, and I started to see the appeal—why so many other ladies I'd met enjoyed this. I did my best not to be distracted by the heat of Sebastian's chest against my back or the feel of his breath on my ear as he gave me little directions and advice, as surely no true lady would think about such things.

In fact, as we neared the end of our ride, his home coming into sight once more, I began to worry that I'd made a mistake. I couldn't imagine Liesl approving of this if she had known, to say nothing of

Idonia. I'd set out to establish my place here, to prove I belonged, and all I'd proven was that I have no idea what things are proper in my new role.

So before we'd even come to a full stop, I untangled myself from Sebastian's arms and my feet from the stirrups and slid off the horse, but I did not land quite on my feet and fell in the mud, no doubt ruining my dress. Yet another mishap.

"Is everything alright?" Sebastian asked, dismounting the horse the way one is supposed to, ending on their own two feet.

"Of course. It's only that I must get back," I said, wiping mud from my hands. "My sister is expecting me." I took the reins from his hands with a jerky motion and attempted to get back on the horse. I never should've dismounted it, but I'd panicked.

Sebastian had taken out a handkerchief for me to use, but I shook my head, and he stuffed it back in his pocket. Then he sighed and cupped his hands against his knee to boost me up, a questioning look in his eyes. I scrambled onto the horse, kicking him into a gallop before I had time to realize I had not thanked Sebastian as I should have. I turned back and waved to him. His silhouette was already fading out of sight, but I saw him lift his hand to wave back.

I let out a long breath, annoyed at myself for such a blunder. The whole thing had been a blunder, really. Why had I thought I was ready for a solo ride away from the stables?

But then I realized: my horse was galloping. I was still secure in the saddle. I trusted him, at least more than I had, and he trusted me. Next time there was a hunting party, I could take him out and join the other ladies. Perhaps even make a friend, like Cristina had suggested. I was one step closer to finding my place here, and thanks to the gardener, of all people. I really must write him a note to express my thanks.

CHAPTER FOURTEEN

Anne's Diary

8 SEPTEMBER

I do not know what's the matter with me. The last few days were rainy, and though the library is full of books that shall perhaps take me a lifetime to read, I felt listless and found myself wandering about the castle with nothing to do. But the weather alone cannot be to blame. Today is sunny again, and I've strolled in the woods for so long that my legs feel ready to drop off, but still, I feel dissatisfied.

And how can I feel that way? Here Liesl and I are surrounded by luxury and the best of everything. All the splendors we dreamt of in the meadow—and many more we could not have imagined—have come true. Why is it, then, that I feel so melancholy?

I wrote to Klaus a few days ago and told him how happy Liesl and I are, but it felt like a lie. Liesl seems happy enough to be mistress of this grand estate, but I . . .

At the last ball, I found myself examining the painted panels on the wall for the first time. There were always such fine gowns to see and foods to try that I hadn't really looked at them before. They are surrounded by gilded wooden carvings and depict scenes of the countryside. A shepherd leaning on his crook, a cowherd in the field with his animals, a goose girl resting beside a pond. Just the sort of life I left behind when I came here. What a strange thing for noblemen to adorn their walls with! They must not understand the hardships of that life. Perhaps everyone wants what they do not have, just as I longed for castles and knights and adventure from our meadow.

Yesterday I thought the problem could be that I am no longer useful. At home, I was useful without even trying—tending our goats, helping Liesl with the spinning, mending and cooking, trading goat's milk in the village—but here, what can I do? Liesl tried, a few days past, to show me how to arrange flowers in the pleasing ways that she does, but it was a hopeless endeavor. She is not as patient with me as she once was, so I let her alone again.

And what use is that, anyway, when Sebastian keeps all the castle's vases filled with whatever blooms are in season? Based on the flowers that adorn so many surfaces in this castle, he might even be more skilled than Liesl.

There are no goats here to tend, but I thought perhaps the cook might put me to use in the kitchen. She is a red-cheeked, plump, merry woman who likes to sing as she works. Her name is Ulla, but everyone calls her Cook. At first, when I asked to help, she seemed a little taken aback. However, when I complimented her cooking as the best I'd ever had—which was an easy compliment to give, since neither Liesl nor I are brilliant cooks—and asked to learn her ways, she warmed right up and set me to work shaping pretzels.

The warmth and familiar smell of baking bread were a comfort. Molding and working the dough, my hands busy and my apron flour-streaked, was the best I had felt in several days. Perhaps there was something to making oneself useful, even within a castle where there's no need for it. Cook told me all about her life and how her grandmother taught her the ways of the kitchen. When she found out I loved fairy tales, I told her a few stories as we worked—Red Riding Hood and the Six Swans and Rapunzel.

I was happy, or as close to it as I had been for quite some time, until I noticed the other servants. They darted in and out of the kitchen, making no effort to hide how they stared at me and whispered behind their hands. As Cook redid most of my pretzels, which were too lopsided for her to accept, and dipped them in the murky lye-and-water mixture so they would turn dark in the oven, I began to feel rather embarrassed. Perhaps it was even more unusual than I had thought for a "lady" to help in the kitchens.

Cook noticed my unease and smiled, even though she'd had to redo nearly every twist I had made. "Pay them no mind, Fraulein," she said in a pitying way.

"What are they whispering about?" I worked sticky bits of dough off my palms and fingers, dropping them on the wooden work surface and trying to seem only casually interested in what the servants thought of me.

"They are silly," Cook said, waving her rolling pin at a pair of maids. They scattered like spooked crows. "So superstitious."

The hairs on the back of my neck stood on end. "Superstitious about what?" I suddenly remembered the rumors Silvia had mentioned, that the castle was haunted. I'd forgotten about it in all the excitement, but I realized now that I hadn't seen anything to make me believe ghosts resided here. Nor had I seen any evidence of Bluebeard's previous wife, the one who had run away. There was only that one time that I doubted, when Idonia scolded me for wandering beneath the castle, and I was so overtired that I imagined a fox had led me there.

Cook frowned as she arranged her dozen perfect pretzels on two trays and lowered them into the oven. She wiped her hands on a towel and didn't look at me for so long that I thought she had decided to ignore my question entirely.

But then she led me to the long table where the staff ate their meals—where I sometimes wished I could eat mine, too. Dinners with Bluebeard and Liesl were so terribly formal, and I was always worried I would make some etiquette error and earn another scathing look from Idonia. Cook placed two teacups down and filled them with hot water from the kettle. Then she sat across from me and began steeping her tea.

"Now," she said, "I shall tell you why the servants whisper about you and your sister, but you must promise not to speak a word of this to the master."

I nodded. I was never alone with the man and hardly spoke two words together to him anyway, even when Liesl and I dined or spent quiet evenings in the library with him.

"You must know that he had another wife before your sister."

Possibly several, if the rumors were to be believed, but I only nodded again.

Cook leaned back in her chair, drawing her teacup and saucer closer to her. "It was nigh on fifteen years ago now," she said. "Or so they tell me. Only a few servants are still here from that time. The master would have been a younger man then, though some claim he hasn't aged a day since. His wife Amalie, God rest her soul, was a delicate little thing, from what I understand—not strong like you." She smiled at me, but I couldn't return it. What good was being strong if one were also clumsy?

When Cook sipped her tea and seemed as if she might not go on, I swallowed nervously. Did I dare ask that which I desperately wanted to know? Cook was perhaps the kindest person I had met since arriving here, and I wanted to trust someone. "What happened to her?"

"She and the master got into some sort of tiff one night. It surprised everyone, since she had never before raised her voice above a whisper. She ran off. There was a mighty storm that night. I heard—oh, it's awful to speak of—but I heard the poor girl drowned in the river."

Cook's lips pressed together, and one small tear escaped the corner of her eye. She brushed it away quickly. "Sorry, love. My heart just aches whenever I think of her, out there on her own. She must not have been quite right in the head to run away like that."

"It's tragic," I agreed as the hairs on the back of my neck rose. "But what does that have to do with superstition?"

"Some of the sillier maids," she said, casting a sharp look toward the doorway, though there was no one there, "believe the castle to be haunted by her. It is an old structure, you know, and makes noise as it settles in the night or as the drafts blow through. They tell all kinds of tales—that the master is cursed or that a curse lays upon any woman who becomes his bride."

"Is there a curse?" I asked, breathless, before I could stop myself.

Her stern look was turned on me now. "Of course not, and I hope I won't hear you talking that way. Ghosts and curses." She made a dismissive noise, shaking her head. "I know you like fairy tales, love, but don't confuse them for what's real."

"Of course not," I said, blushing. But there was something unsettled inside me now. I didn't want to think about "ghosts and curses," but what made the servants see them if there was nothing to it? I hadn't seen evidence that implied anything of the kind, but I had only lived here a fortnight. If the servants who called the castle home believed something was amiss, how could I dismiss their worries?

And why had Amalie run off, really?

Whether it is all the maids' imaginations or not, this castle holds secrets and shadows. I pray that whatever befell the other wife—or *wives*—will not touch my sister or me. I think of the fox incident again, and I doubt myself even more. Do I imagine dangers that don't exist, or are there hidden things here which must be uncovered?

"Now drink your tea, love, and do not worry yourself over the past. I think you've had enough baking for now. Come back a week from today, and I'll teach you how to make honey cakes."

I resolved, for now, to do as she said. I do not want to anger Idonia again, and I am afraid my urge to be of use will get me into trouble. Amalie's time here is long past—I probably could not yet walk when she disappeared—and I should let it lie.

And so now I am back here, in the library, feeling useless and listless once again. The books do not amuse me, the walk through the woods tired me but did not fill up my soul like it should have. This is longer than I have ever been apart from Father or any of my brothers. I do not know when I shall next see them, or if they will recognize me when they do. I hardly recognize myself in the many mirrors that hang around the castle, with my fine clothes and elaborate hairstyles. Idonia's lessons have even ensured I walk differently than I did before.

I long to run through our meadow barefoot again, picking wildflowers and arranging them in a little cup at the center of our age-worn table, surrounded by those I love.

Being barefoot at all no longer seems proper, and the gardens and castle are bursting with flowers, with no need for me to lift a finger.

What splendors this palace holds, but what small pleasures I miss from home.

Chapter Fifteen

Letter from Liesl

9 September

Dearest Mother,

I've been married a fortnight now, and I find myself wishing you were here more and more. There's so much about the world that I thought I knew. Each day, there are at least a dozen questions that I want to ask you. Everything here is harder than I expected it would be.

There are a great many things to learn, including the varied and perplexing etiquette of the gentry. I do not mind these so much. They are expected, after all, and sometimes it feels as if I have entered a whole other world. Anne struggles more than I do, and I grow impatient with her. It is a small price to pay for the life we have now. It doesn't help that I cannot share my struggles with her, and must try to make her believe me happy with my husband. At times,

I cannot help but envy her and think of all I have sacrificed for her gain.

We are no strangers to hard work, but I have never felt such pressure to be exactly what another wants of me. To be flawless. Sometimes I feel I am just another one of my husband's fine treasures and furnishings, something to represent his prosperity and be displayed to his many guests. We rarely speak beyond his few instructions about the running of the estate and the grand events I must arrange.

On the surface, it does not sound as if I should struggle, but perhaps, when summed together, it is all too much. A strange malaise has come over me. Uncanny sounds and happenings surround me in my room, and I struggle to sleep at night. It is almost as if—but no, I do not want you to think that I am unbalanced. Perhaps this drafty, ancient castle has given me some peculiar ailment. I only wish I could trust my senses, that I did not have to fear for my mind.

The bright spot in all this—besides the stipend to support the family, of course—is my chance to find Anne an advantageous match. She can still have the future which I once dreamt might be mine. Several young nobles are interested in her, and I'm sure it is only a matter of time before she has an offer of marriage of her own.

I miss you more than words can say.

With all my love,

Liesl

CHAPTER SIXTEEN

Anne's Diary

10 SEPTEMBER

Before Bluebeard came to our village, I had never given much thought to betrothal or marriage. I'd felt so young, still. But now that Liesl is grown and married I feel as if I have grown up too. In this dazzling palace, amidst Liesl's wedding celebrations and with multiple suitors, I admit that I do not think of much else.

There are two young nobles who have expressed intentions of courting me. Franz is the future lord of an estate not far from here. He is quite a serious young man, but a marvelous dancer. His physique is of the tall, dark, and handsome variety, which I must say is pleasant. We have talked a little of books, though I do not think he has read quite so many as I have. It is a little disappointing, as until coming here, the only books I'd read were the ones Silvia loaned me on my visits, whereas I'm sure Franz has a whole library at home.

My other suitor is Gustav, second son of a large and prosperous estate two days' journey from here. He is not as tall or dark or handsome as Franz, but he is quick with a smile and always makes me laugh. There is something charming about his round face, ruddy cheeks, and sparkling blue eyes. Gustav has even written me a poem! He is not a great poet, but it was quite sweet nonetheless.

I would not feel right about delighting in these admirers' attentions if my sister did not seem so content. We made up a few days ago. She apologized for her impatience with me and mentioned how tired all the excitement lately has made her. I forgave her immediately, of course, though I have not offered my help since, as we have been getting along well enough once again and I do not wish to ruin it.

The melancholy that has afflicted me the past few days does not seem so strong for her, and she is settling in well with her less-than-handsome husband. She told me yesterday that he can be quite charming at times and that she thinks his beard is really not so very blue nor he so boorish. She has already become a beloved hostess to our many guests. I am proud of her, and hope that, should I be wed in a few years, I could do as well as she.

This morning, however, Liesl was a bit somber. When I inquired after the cause of her downcast expression, she assured me it was nothing. I suspect that the homesickness I have suffered may be starting to affect her, too. It has been difficult to adapt to being without our father, and the usual hustle and bustle of our five brothers in and out of our small cottage, and the villagers who have known us our whole lives. Perhaps Bluebeard will take us back for a visit in a few months for Christmas. We could bring them gifts as extravagant as those Bluebeard received for the wedding. Else they could make the journey here to see his fine estate.

I long to see how the little goats born this spring have grown up, and to have tea with Silvia and hear the village news. I wonder what I should give to read a book borrowed from her and Warner, sitting beneath my twisted tree on the hill, enjoying the sweeping view of the countryside again?

Perhaps it is best not to dwell on these memories. Liesl is low-spirited enough today; I will be full of cheer for her and take my turn for sadness when she is feeling better. I think I shall see if she'd like to take a stroll in the gardens. The sunshine should rally our spirits. The gardens are far larger and more elaborate than ours at home, with flowers in place of crops, but today I confess that I would prefer a stroll through our meadow.

Well, I did take Liesl on a stroll through the gardens, but it did not go quite as planned.

We admired the lovely flowers and the clever patterns Sebastian had made with their colors, and I do think it was cheering Liesl up. The fresh air and sunlight surely did her good, too, and she did not seem so weak as she sometimes does inside the castle. Her hand was linked through my arm, and I bore a little of her weight, which was unusual. Perhaps she is only overtired from all the late nights of dancing.

We talked of little, insignificant things until we broached the subject of the recent festivities.

"You had some enthusiastic dancing partners last night," Liesl said, grinning at me in a mischievous way and arching an eyebrow. "Which do you prefer, Herr Franz or Herr Gustav?"

I laughed, my cheeks warm. "Each has some allure, I confess. But Liesl, you cannot think that I am ready for marriage yet. Or that—a far greater hardship to bear—I want to leave you so soon?"

I hoped to make her laugh, but she only grew silent and pensive as we started another turn about the lily garden. "I would miss you dearly, there is no question of that," she said eventually. "But Anne—if I could see you happily settled, everything will have been worth it."

My heart sank at her words. Was being married to Bluebeard truly so awful that she needed me to make a good match, too, in order to bear it? She'd seemed so happy planning the balls, but now I wondered if her intention was not to be the ideal hostess for Bluebeard but to play matchmaker for me.

In the softest voice I could manage, I asked, "Is it really so difficult with him, Liesl? I know you did not care for him at first, but I hoped that with time—"

"Hush, Anne." She gripped my arm and gave me a thin smile. "Of course I care for him; he is my husband."

How many questions I wanted to ask! How worried I am for her. But it is not like growing up together at home. There is a wall between us now, and so many things of which we cannot speak, which are improper for me to know. It is difficult, and made more difficult because we used to share everything with each other.

Hoping that a slight change in scenery might loosen her tongue, I led her out of the late-summer lily garden and toward a walled one I had meant to explore further. There were some marvelous flowers there, but I did not know the names of most of them.

"Oh, how lovely," Liesl said, kneeling beside a small bush with clusters of pink starburst blooms. Next to them was a row of stems hung with delicate white bell-shaped flowers, and another row of oddly shaped flowers in a deep, rich purple.

There were so many types, but I could not discern a common pattern in color or shape, the way the rest of the gardens were arranged.

"Ah, here's one I recognize," I said, bending to smell the cluster of trumpet-shaped purple flowers on a tall stem. "Foxglove."

I scanned the garden once again, looking for a thread to tie them together, but there were blooms of every shape and shade, and even a few plants that did not look as if they would flower at all. I only saw one more that I recognized: the yellow-centered, blue disks of morning glories. I was still puzzling over the theme when Idonia entered the walled garden, wearing her usual black dress and carrying a woven basket on her arm. She looked surprised to see us.

"Good afternoon, Idonia," Liesl said, smiling sweetly.

"What are you doing here?"

Her words were sharp, and Liesl flinched as if Idonia had struck her. When Liesl spoke, her eyes were wide, and her lips trembled. "We were only taking a stroll through the gardens."

"You would do well to steer clear of *this* garden on your rambles, Mistress."

I raised my chin and crossed my arms, feeling my nostrils flare with my temper. "Why should the mistress of the castle be denied access to *any* of its gardens?"

Idonia's mouth fell open at my impertinence. "These are my personal collection, and I do not wish to have them disturbed."

I could not argue with that but didn't wish to back down—especially after the incident with the fox. After all, if that were the only reason, she could have explained it in a kinder way. We had certainly not "disturbed" any of her plants. While Idonia and I glared daggers at each other amidst the flowers, Liesl stood and cleared her throat.

"My apologies, Idonia," she said, looking down at her hands as she straightened her skirts. "We did not mean to intrude on your private garden. It shall not happen again. Come, Anne."

I did not wish to leave, but Liesl's pleading look dragged me away. Idonia had made her feel embarrassed and small, and I am still not sure I can forgive that, especially as she also must have noticed how Liesl has been lately.

Liesl did not speak for quite some time as I led her back through the gardens we had already explored. When she did, it was a meaningless comment about the weather, but her voice betrayed that she had been near tears, and another fierce wave of anger at Idonia washed over me.

I tried to coax her to take a longer stroll with me into the woods, as they are quite pretty, and I have started to grow familiar with their trails. We got so far as the field in which the horses were grazing today, and Liesl said she was too tired to go on. We leaned on the fence and watched a pair of muscular stallions with shining black coats. My favorite horse, the dappled gray gelding, grazed at the far end of the pasture.

Again, there was a long silence in which Liesl said nothing, twisting her ring on her finger. In the sunlight, it winked green and purple before returning to its customary near-black sapphire. Finally, in a quiet voice, Liesl said, "Please do not make this hard for me, Anne."

I am sure I have never felt so guilty. Her words seemed to imply even more: "this is already hard for me, do not make it harder." My face heated with shame. How have I gone so far off-track from my promise to keep her safe and happy? She is not as happy as she once was, and as for her safety . . . I still know almost nothing about Bluebeard's past.

Well, no more. Herr Franz and Herr Gustav and everyone else will have to wait. My sister needs me.

"I promise," I told her, also promising myself to do much more than she asked. I would do anything for my sister—even discover the truth about Bluebeard's other wives.

CHAPTER SEVENTEEN

Gustav's Poem

I spied you, an angel, across the ballroom floor.

You have no wings, but you still soar,

And it is only you whom I adore.

Your dress was lace,

You danced with grace,

A lovely smile upon your face.

Would you make me happy forevermore,

With your hand and your *amour*?

- G

CHAPTER EIGHTEEN

Anne's Diary

12 SEPTEMBER

I ran into Sebastian today. He was pulling weeds from the tulip beds while I was out for a stroll.

"I should have thanked you." The words burst from my mouth the moment I saw him. "For the riding lesson," I clarified.

"You did," he said, squinting up at me and into the sunlight from where he knelt on the ground. "I got your note."

"Right," I said. "But I mean, at the time. It's just, I think I was embarrassed. Because I was so bad with the horse."

"You were," he said, smirking. I reflected, not for the first time, that he was pleasing to look at, even without the finery that Herr Franz and Herr Gustav and my other suitors wore. "But you've improved. I saw you out the other day."

"Yes," I agreed. "I think I have. It's hard when—well, it has been difficult. I wasn't born to this."

"You'll be foxhunting before you know it."

The fox below the castle entered my mind, and my smile faded a little. "I don't think so, but at least I won't bring shame on my sister now."

Sebastian stuck his trowel upright in the dirt and wiped his hands on his trousers. His work shirt was open a little at the collar, and I tried not to stare at the curves of his collarbone or the bare skin of his chest. "When we met the other day, you started to ask me something," he said. "What was it?"

"Oh," I said, flicking my eyes away. "I just had questions about some of the flowers."

"Well, you've come to the right place," he said, standing and sweeping his arms out over the tulip beds and toward the distant rose garden. "Ask away."

We strolled together in the gardens—not with my hand on his arm, as I have done with some of the noble boys, but quietly in step with each other. He gave me names for the flowers I did not know already, and I've made sure to commit them to memory. The other day Liesl asked me the name of the flowers which adorn parts of the castle and many of the garden walls, the ones with great trailing bunches of purple flowers. With all the books I've read on the subject, I felt quite embarrassed that I did not know. But I shall remember now: wisteria.

The strange thing about Sebastian, however—the thing that left such an impression that I felt the need to write about our encounter, though it was so brief—was what he said just before we parted.

"It was nice to see you again, Fraulein," he said and gave a little half-bow.

"Please call me Anne," I reminded him. I'd asked all the servants to address me so, deciding to rank my own comfort over Idonia's disapproval in this one case.

He did not respond to that, but as I turned to go, he grasped the sleeve of my dress to make me face him again. He leaned in close and said, "I feel compelled to give you a few words of advice. This castle has dangers and secrets that I hope you shall never know. You and your sister must do whatever Idonia says, and avoid any curiosity about what has happened here before."

I was so shaken at the time—not by his words so much as by the solemn tone in which he said them, and the feel of his breath on my neck and ear—that I simply thanked him and left. Had I my wits about me, I would have told him that saying such a thing only ensured that I was more curious than ever about the castle's history, and especially about Bluebeard's missing wives. And I shall certainly *never* unquestioningly do what Idonia says. I do not trust her at all after the way she spoke to us in her secret garden, and so I suppose I cannot trust Sebastian either.

Liesl does not know about my time with Sebastian or his warning. I do not think I shall tell her. Her spirits have been so low of late, and I do not wish to distress her further. After Sebastian's words, I am afraid for her. Every day she grows thinner, paler, and more disinterested in anything I offer her. But I must persevere. Perhaps today I can convince her to go for a ride. Or if that is too much for her, perhaps she can be persuaded to take a turn about the garden, and I can tell her the new names of the flowers I have just learned.

I have been trying to learn more of Bluebeard's past, but so far, I've found nothing to say that his other wives existed. The paintings of beautiful women in the Great Gallery are all so old that they must be his ancestors and not his wives. There is no painting of Amalie—perhaps they were not married long enough to have her portrait taken. But still, it seems strange.

None of the servants, aside from Cook, have mentioned the wives, though if something else tragic happened, I suppose they would avoid speaking of it. The castle has such a timelessness to it that it's hard to imagine, even if Bluebeard had had a dozen other wives, that they would have put much of their own mark on it. Liesl has certainly not ventured to change anything to her liking yet.

For now, I shall have to content myself with finding out more about Idonia. I am more curious about her than ever after Sebastian's admonishment to listen to her.

I started by asking Cristina what she knew of her. Unfortunately, it was very little. She said Idonia has been with the castle longer than any of the other staff, and that she demands perfection from those beneath her. I am trying not to be frustrated, but those seem like things I could have guessed.

Sebastian was no help at all. I found him, in the conservatory this time, and asked him about Idonia and her garden as subtly as I could—which must not have been subtle at all, because he sighed in an exasperated way.

"This is exactly what you should not do." He was tending to a shelf of orchids with a tin watering can and had seemed friendly and happy to see me until I asked him a question. "I asked you to check your curiosity."

"How can I, though, when such terrible rumors followed Bluebeard to our village?" I whispered.

"If you heard such frightening things of him," Sebastian said, his voice carefully even, "why would your sister accept him, or you agree to come with her?" He moved to another shelf but turned back to raise an eyebrow at me.

"My sister fell in love with him." I was flushed, and the lie burned on my tongue.

I could not tell if he believed me, and I wasn't sure why I cared. He was only the gardener. The gardener who clearly knew *something*, else why would he have asked me to listen to Idonia?

Pursing my lips, I moved closer to him and said in a low voice, "Please, Sebastian, just tell me one thing: to your knowledge, is my sister in danger?"

He did not respond right away, instead watering a row of young citrus trees before checking the leaves of a bromeliad and placing the watering can on the floor. He turned to me, and the light streaming in through the glass walls made his gray-blue eyes glow like glass. "No," he said finally. "Right now, I do not believe she is. But"—he leaned closer so that I caught his warm, earthy scent—"if the master leaves, beware. That's all I will say. I daresay I've said too much already."

"If the master leaves . . ." I repeated. If Bluebeard left, Idonia must oversee the running of the castle. Well, my sister would be in charge, but I had yet to see her disagree with anything Idonia wished. Was she, then, the source of the danger? He had warned me to do what she says . . .

"Please, stop," Sebastian said gently, and I thought, for a strange moment, he might take my hand. "I can see you worrying and giving too much weight to my words. All is well."

"What's in Idonia's garden?" I asked, giving up on my fruitless attempts at subtlety. I crossed my arms and locked eyes with him, rather like I had with Idonia the other day.

Sebastian was again slow to respond. He adjusted the ties that held an orchid stem to its support, and I grew impatient, afraid he was going to ignore my question altogether. "What Idonia grows in her garden is her business alone," he said finally. "I do not tend it—but I assure you it is nothing that should give you cause for distress."

There was a subtle emphasis on the word "you" that made me immediately anxious for Liesl. But then he picked up the watering can and made to exit the conservatory. He turned back to me and said, "Will that be all, Fraulein?"

"Anne," I said reflexively.

A smile tugged at the corner of his mouth. "Will that be all, Fraulein Anne?"

Clearly, it was a dismissal, though I should have been the one dismissing him. I raised my chin and managed a somewhat confident, "Yes."

I was left in the warm conservatory, yet again with no leads on Bluebeard's past or whatever Idonia was hiding.

Chapter Nineteen

Bluebeard's Diary | Renate

5 February, 8th Year of King Lukas III

E leven years, it has been, since I extended my life. Aside from my lengthening beard, my appearance has not changed. However, now that it has been more than a decade, I do not feel so strong and hale as I did after the ritual. I suppose it must be repeated, now and again, to replenish my strength, though the witch in the grotto did not tell me how often, and she has long since moved on from my lands.

My one regret is what happened with Cacilie. She could not see my wisdom—she was not ready for this greatness, this power. I would not undo what I have done for the world, but I have often turned an envious eye on my fellow noblemen and the pretty women they wed. Cacilie outshone them all, and I know I cannot love anyone now as I once did her. I am somewhere above the human plane, and as such, I cannot truly give my heart to anyone beneath me.

But why should I deprive myself of the beauty and care of a young woman?

I have pondered this question over the last year, and, as a man of action, I also looked for a woman worthy of my wealth and consequence. After careful consideration, I have found one. Persuading her to marry me was simple. Had only my wealth been in my favor, it would have been simple enough, but with tales of my lovely first wife, it was easy. I had only to cast myself in the role of grieving, brooding widower, and she believed me to have a heart like that of any other man.

Renate will look splendid on my arm. She is all delicate wrists and porcelain skin and red hair that glows gold in the candlelight. She plays piano and sings like an angel and does not ask too many questions. She is perfect.

But after what happened with Cacilie, I must proceed differently. Renate must never know the source of my power; she must be content to obey whatever I tell her. To ensure she is, I have devised a test for after we are married. If she succeeds, she will enjoy her mortal life in power and prosperity. If not—well, she shall be more easily dealt with than Cacilie, in any case.

17 Days Later

I had high hopes, but Renate failed me. Ah, well. I shall once again be the grief-stricken widower among my acquaintance, and I must admit that suits me. Besides, I feel decades younger once again and as invincible as ever. I should not need to repeat the ritual for quite some time.

It is strange. I have noticed a small difference today. My beard has changed color slightly, so that in sunlight, it has a blue sheen. All else is the same. No matter. It will add an air of intrigue about me, and it is not as if anyone would suspect what it means.

CHAPTER TWENTY

Anne's Diary

16 September

Liesl and I spent a pleasant afternoon in the library yesterday. As autumn is beginning, it often grows dark before dinner now. My eyes grew tired of reading by candlelight, and I walked to the windows. They face eastward, and little light makes it through the colored segments of glass, but I thought I spotted a figure down below us. A man in dark clothes, standing still at the edge of the woods, his face upturned as if toward us.

I glanced at Liesl, who held her lacework close, concentrating. Even with the warm glow of the candles and the hearth fire, she looked pale, and I didn't wish to alarm her. I examined the dark figure, peering through one of the small yellow pieces in the stained-glass mosaic of the window. It was too stout to be Sebastian, but I did not know who else might be lurking about the property at this hour, and wondered if I should alert Bluebeard.

But as I watched, the figure—now lit by the glow of a few fireflies hovering around it—did not move. I realized it was not a person at all but a statue or some other monument. It seemed the castle and its grounds held no end of secrets, and I was determined to explore this one. I could not shake the uneasy foreboding it gave me, even after I knew it was not a nighttime prowler.

"Do you smell that?" Liesl asked me while I was still at the window. She set her embroidery in her lap and sniffed the air.

I did. The scent was strong and permeated the room. "Roses?"

"But there are no flowers in here."

I went to the door and poked my head into the hall, thinking perhaps one of the servants was refreshing flower arrangements and had walked by, leaving the floral scent in their wake. There was no one there.

"How strange," Liesl said as she picked up her lace again and found her place. "What a drafty old castle this is."

It certainly was old and drafty, but I did not see how such a strong scent could be blown in by a draft. Between that and what I'd seen out the window, I felt unsettled, though I could not say exactly why.

So this morning, after breakfast, I set out on a brisk walk to the east of the castle. It was a cool morning, and a fine mist lay over the land. From the library, I had thought this place was only the edge of the wilderness. The trees beyond it stretched back as far as the eye could see. But now that I was up close, I could make out a low stone wall, half hidden by brambles, and followed it until I came to a wrought iron gate. It was not locked, so I pulled it open with a grunt of effort and passed through. It squealed on its old hinges, then slammed shut behind me, and I jumped. I cleared my throat, straightened my hair, and continued, thankful that no one had seen me spooked by a gate.

A few steps in, I laughed at myself for being so silly last night. It was only a cemetery. Of course an estate like this, in the hands of the same family for so many generations, must have somewhere to bury their dead.

The figure I'd seen last night was a stone statue of an angel. There were several other tall headstones, most shaped like crosses, and other, far simpler ones worn down by time. Moss covered many, and the air felt damp and smelled like rain. I knelt next to one of the stones, mindful not to dirty my dress, and carefully moved vines away, uncovering the inscription. It was a woman named Cacilie, and she'd died over seventy years ago.

It struck me then that if Bluebeard had wives before Liesl, and if they'd died, they must be buried here. Of late, I'd neglected my plan to find out more about his wives because I had not known how to continue. Gravestones were surely a good source of clues—one I should have thought of before.

Quickly, I moved along the uneven rows of stones, peeling up moss and pushing away leaves and dirt wherever needed. I searched for women who had died in the last fifty years, who perhaps had Bluebeard's surname or an epitaph naming her his wife or his love. One name I was sure to find: Amalie's. I frowned, realizing I'd had to learn her name from the cook. I'd never heard Bluebeard say her name, though he'd mentioned his last wife when he asked Father for his permission to court us. How long ago, and in what a different world, that moment seems now.

By the time I had read every inscription, my dress was muddy, and my fingers trembled from running over so many cold gravestones. There was no Amalie, no other wives. In fact, there were not any recent deaths. Most had died over a hundred years ago, many two or three hundred years past.

I turned and looked at the angel, positioned in the center of the cemetery, as I contemplated this. She, too, showed the wear of many years. Her details were lost to time, but her serene expression and gracefully outstretched hands remained. A few lighter marks marred her stone, including a tear-like one on her cheek.

If no one had been buried here recently, perhaps that meant there was another cemetery on the grounds. Still, I felt uneasy. Amalie should be here, and if there had been other wives, they should be, too. And what of Bluebeard's parents? Were they not laid to rest here among their ancestors?

On my way out of the graveyard, I passed Sebastian and nodded to him. His sharp eyes picked up the stains where my knees had sunk into the dirt and my muddied hands, but he said nothing. He pursed his lips and bowed, then glanced at the castle, his expression worried.

I suppose he realized I was investigating the past, just what he'd warned me against. Or he was considering what Idonia would say when she saw my dress. The thought worried me so much that I cleaned it myself before joining Liesl for luncheon in the jewel-box sitting room.

I was silly, earlier, when I saw Sebastian and did not ask him if there were other graves on the grounds. I was a little shaken, as I suppose most people are whenever reminded of death and their own mortality. After our conversation the other day, I wasn't at all sure he would tell me anything, but I didn't see how asking could hurt.

The wall surrounding Idonia's garden seemed an ideal spot—not only could I wait for Sebastian to cross my path while he went about his gardening duties, but I would be sure to notice if Idonia visited and harvested any of her plants. The fog from this morning had cleared as the sun warmed the land, and it was such a lovely day that I decided to choose a book from the library and read it in the dappled sunlight beneath the elm tree there.

When Sebastian finally came my way, I forgot all the sly plans I had made to get information out of him. He smiled at me and I closed the book gently, marking my place with my thumb. Sebastian stopped and leaned on his shovel.

"What are you reading?"

"An adventure novel," I said, my mind too full of questions to offer more. Then I took a deep breath and asked, "Where is Amalie buried?"

Sebastian's expression shuttered, and his friendly tone turned dark. "How do you know about her?"

I stood and crossed my arms, the book dangling from my hands. "Bluebeard mentioned her himself. Why shouldn't I know about her?"

"I'm serious, Fraulein."

"I'm serious, too," I said, trying to make myself taller. "There are rumors of Bluebeard having other wives, and I'm worried—"

"And well you should be," he hissed, glancing from side to side. "If you want my advice, it's this: leave here as soon as you can. It is not safe for you. I thought it might be, if you heeded my warnings, but clearly, you cannot."

"What about my sister?"

He grimaced. "It may be too late for her."

"What? How can you say—?"

"She will be fine if you stop digging into the past. Swear to me that you will leave it alone."

I sighed and uncrossed my arms. "I cannot 'leave it alone.' If I knew just one thing, then perhaps I could—"

"What one thing?" His expression was guarded, and his hand gripped the handle of the shovel tightly.

I leaned in and whispered, "Tell me where Amalie is buried."

"Fine," he said. "I'll tell you: she wasn't."

"How . . . ?"

"You can't bury someone if they're never found." He cut me off with a gesture as I began to protest. "No more questions. I've said far too much. But please, for your own good and your sister's, stop this." Then he shouldered the shovel and left.

As I walked back to the castle, the air grew cold and I shivered. It must have been some effect of the stone walls, trapping air that could not be warmed by the sun. My one thought was that speaking to Sebastian again had not been a complete waste. I knew a little more than I did before. He had verified Cook's information. Amalie existed; she had been married to Bluebeard more than fifteen years ago; and most chilling of all: she was still missing.

CHAPTER TWENTY-ONE

Anne's Diary

22 SEPTEMBER

I found a special place today. I was coming back from my walk through the forest west of the castle. Liesl did not join me—indeed, she joins me less and less often on my daily rambles. She was quite pale this morning, so I made sure to order tea for her before I left and urged her to eat a little. I suppose rest was better for her than overexerting herself on a long walk with me.

There is a route through the woods that is a favorite of mine, as I often spot a doe and her two fawns along it. I walk it almost daily now. As I returned today, I decided to take a turn around the castle before going indoors. Today was lovely—chilly, but the sun was bright and the wind was gentle. The trees have begun to turn color, and the smell of dry leaves permeates the air. Each day I find little differences in the woods that are well worth seeing. I only wish Liesl could join me more often.

As old as the castle is, many of its masters have added onto it during their time. Along the north side of the castle is a low wall whose battlements are in disrepair. They have crumbled from neglect, perhaps because they are no longer needed. Bluebeard, at least, has focused his energies on the main castle with its lavish living quarters.

I walked along this wall to extend my time outdoors. My usual way took me along the west wall to the main south entrance, so it was a nice change. As I walked, my attention was drawn to fireflies glowing against the backdrop of a hill at the edge of the woods. I frowned in puzzlement. It was far too early in the day for fireflies. I went closer to see for myself that they were not actually will-o'-the-wisps or something I had imagined. Always, the fox incident is at the back of my mind, ready to make me distrust whatever I see.

They were indeed fireflies, but as I drew closer to them, what caught my attention was something at the top of the hill. It was not a natural portion of the forest, as I had thought, but an unkempt garden of sorts, hemmed in by gnarled hedges and iron gates. I circled the base of the hill, searching for the easiest path to scale it, and found a stone footpath that meandered up its slope. It must not have been used in some time, for the stones were nearly buried beneath moss, fallen leaves and other debris.

As I followed the path, I caught the strong scent of roses, as I had the other night in the library with Liesl, and paused. There could very well be roses at the top, but why should I smell them here, surrounded by grass and woods and with the strong autumn breeze blowing my hair around me?

I looked back at the castle and appreciated the view. I was used to seeing it close up, but there was a certain loveliness to its faded brick towers and red-shuttered windows when one beheld the whole castle at once. Firelight made the windows of the drawing-room glow, so Liesl must have been working there, either on her new lace piece or on plans with Idonia. When I turned back, the fireflies had vanished.

I shook my head, not wanting to dwell on that or doubt my mind. I was nearly to the top of the hill anyway. There I found mismatched bits of iron gate and brick wall losing their battle with the ivy. The vegetation inside the wall was overgrown, as if no one had tended it for quite some time. But amidst thorny brambles and weeds, I glimpsed delicate black flowers with red-edged petals.

As I worked my way deeper into the heart of the garden, mindful that my skirts did not snag on any thorns or branches, I glimpsed even more blossoms, and thought I could see what it once was—how the paths were laid out and where different types of flowers grew together.

"I wondered when you would find this place."

I jumped at the sound of Sebastian's voice, my hand fluttering to my heart, but by the time he finished speaking, I had composed myself. "And what, exactly, is 'this place?'"

I kept my chin high and tried to look at the garden in the appraising way Bluebeard looks at everything. Moments ago, a look of wonder had been on my face, and for once, I didn't want to be the poor, awestruck goatherd. In hindsight, I probably looked even more ridiculous trying to imitate Bluebeard.

"It's a dead place," Sebastian said, scraping his boot along the gravel of a neglected path. "It belonged to someone who died long before either of us were born."

A chill ran down my spine, but I kept from shuddering and scolded myself for being silly. Though tangled vines and ivy had tried to snuff out all the other plants, roses and lilies emerged from the vines. "It is not dead," I said. "It's merely unloved." I reached out and plucked a black rose, twirling the stem between my fingers. "I wonder how you, the gardener, could have let it grow wild like this."

I was not careful of the rose's thorns, and one pricked me. I inhaled sharply and watched the crimson blood bead on my fingertip. Sebastian, suddenly beside me, withdrew a handkerchief and placed it gently in my hand.

"It is not my choice which gardens are maintained and which are neglected," he said quietly.

I turned to him. "Are you the only gardener in Bluebeard's employ?"

Surely it was far too much for one person, but he confirmed it with a nod.

"And whose choice was it to let this garden go? Bluebeard's or Idonia's?"

"I believe they agreed on this matter."

The vines pulled on my skirts as I took a few steps further into the garden and knelt to push aside strands of ivy, revealing an ink-colored pansy. From this angle, I could see hidden stems of hollyhock that were either black or a maroon so deep they looked it. "Were all the flowers here black?"

"Yes."

In a softer voice, I dared to ask, "This garden belonged to one of them, didn't it? One of the other wives."

He let out a slow breath and nodded. "Yes, but it was long ago. My father, God rest his soul, told me."

"I'm sorry," I said. "About your father, I mean." Sebastian said nothing, so I asked, "And why was this garden not maintained all these years?"

"The master did not care whether it was tended or not. I am not sure he much cares whether the gardens near the castle are maintained either, besides the tulip beds with the rarest bulbs. He uses them so little, but I have tried to keep them up because of the pride my father took in them."

"That's why you've stayed?" I asked. "After your father . . . you could have gone anywhere." I tried to imagine it. Being so tragically alone, but also free to go anywhere. To remake oneself.

He gazed down at the castle. "I did think of leaving," he said softly. "But something kept me here. My father's legacy, perhaps. I couldn't let his life's work fade away. He knew how to use plants to make people breathe deeply, to feel fresh and alive and whole. I've tried to do the same. I cannot say I've always managed it or that I have his skill, but I like to think that without me, the castle and all its gardens might feel more like this one."

"It seems such a shame," I said, finally standing and brushing the dirt and leaves from my skirt. "It must have been beautiful, once. I think it could be again."

Sebastian caught my eye. "If someone were to love it? You said it was only unloved."

I nodded.

"Are you asking me to maintain it, Fraulein?"

It felt so strange that I could ask someone to do such work, and they would have to obey. "Please call me Anne," I said. "And I am asking only if you are willing to help me bring this garden back to life. I shall be happy to work the soil myself again, but I don't believe I can do it alone."

"Very well. I shall help you." A slow half-smile spread over his face. "Anne."

It was the first time he'd called me by my name with no "Fraulein," and my heart did a strange little flutter at the sound of it.

CHAPTER TWENTY-TWO

Anne's Diary

26 SEPTEMBER

Sebastian and I have worked in the garden, side by side, every day since I discovered it. It has been refreshing to spend so much time in the fresh air, the sun on my back and my hands in the earth. To work hard and see a place transformed by it—this is something I had never realized before was a blessing, and something I've missed since coming here.

Perhaps it is not appropriate of me to be dirtying my hands anymore. When I asked Idonia where my old dress had gone, she said it had been thrown out, and my heart sank. It was only an ill-fitting dress, and I'd had no need of it since my arrival. I only needed it now to keep my finer clothes clean, so surely it being thrown out should not have affected me as it did. It was not my past *life* that was thrown out for being unfit for the castle, after all. Only a dress.

I was a little afraid to ask Idonia for new dresses—as, indeed, I am always a little fearful to speak to her—but she did not scold me or claim I must always dress as a lady now, as I thought she might. Instead, she asked, "Dresses suitable for gardening? Whatever for?"

"Seb—the gardener," I corrected, afraid she might not approve of me fraternizing with one of the servants. "I have asked the gardener to restore that neglected garden on the hill, and I plan to help him with it."

Idonia's gaze went glassy, as if she stared at something far away. "The garden on the hill," she repeated, in almost a whisper.

"Yes. The one with all the black flowers."

After a moment that stretched so long I almost gave up and told her I would not dirty my hands after all, she seemed to collect herself. Straightening her spine and clearing her throat, she said brusquely, "Of course. It has been neglected long enough." But she did not meet my eyes with her piercing ones the way she normally does. "I shall order you two simple dresses, Fraulein. They should arrive in a few days. Now please go about your business. I am very busy."

She did not have to tell me twice. In the meantime, I have borrowed one of Cristina's day dresses, though it is laughably short on me and rather too large in the top.

I have not told Liesl what Sebastian and I are up to, partly because I expect she will disapprove of me spending time alone with a servant boy, and partly because I want to surprise her when it is all cleaned up. I do not think she even knows that it exists, so what a nice gift I shall give her when she sees it brought back to its full glory.

The leaves are dropping, and we must hurry to finish before the first frost comes. Sebastian thinks it shall only be one or two days more. When it ends, I think I shall ask if I can join him, sometimes, and work the other gardens, too. It would give me a purpose here, and perhaps that purpose could be twofold; in time, I hope to pull more information from him.

I've learned a great deal about him over the last few days, and he has asked me about myself so much that I suppose he knows nearly as much about me now.

There are things he even seems to know without me telling him. Like one morning, when I confided in him about my desire to write novels. I haven't even spoken to Liesl of that dream since we arrived, and I was afraid he might laugh and think me silly.

Instead, he grinned and said, "I thought as much."

"How?" I asked. "How could you know?"

He smirked, pointing to the ink stains on my forefinger and thumb. I curled my hand into a fist to hide them.

"Oh."

"I've seen you writing a few times," he added. His slim, sure fingers plucked out weeds from around the stepping-stones. "In the library or by the rose garden."

"That's just a journal. It's silly, I suppose, but sometimes I just feel I *must* write."

"Not at all. I think it means there's so much up here,"—he tapped his temple—"that it spills over onto paper."

"Yes," I said, a little unnerved at how clearly he saw me. "That's exactly how it feels sometimes."

That was far from the only thing he seemed to understand about me. His mother died when he was young, just as mine had, but his father also died when he was twelve years old. He had to continue as the castle gardener to get by. I tried to imagine that—having no mother or father or siblings, and working under the cold figures of Idonia and Bluebeard at such a young age. It seems that now, at least, he has settled into his role and views this as his home. I hope I shall, too, someday.

It's clear he takes pride in the gardens and knows a great deal about working them. He was able to identify all the plants in the secret garden, even some of the stranger ones that have grown up over the years. Together we have pulled weeds up by the roots, pruned over-grown shrubs, and fought back the brambles. Several paths through the garden have emerged, and it is much easier to navigate now.

"What will the mistress think?" Sebastian asked me this morning. The sun had come out and cleared the fog, and he wiped the sweat from his brow with his shirt sleeve.

Despite her occasional melancholy and sickly days, Liesl has embraced her role so well these last weeks that it was no longer strange to think of her as the mistress of the castle. How could I have imagined that one day she would be ordering servants around with the same big-sister tone she takes so often with me?

"She will love it," I told Sebastian, smiling.

He smiled back, and warmth coursed through me to my fingers and toes. His black hair shone in the sunlight, and his long limbs moved with an ease he did not possess in the other gardens. It seems

Sebastian, too, is enlivened by being on the hill. Out of the castle's shadow.

My only disappointment is that I have learned no more of Blue-beard's past during all this time with Sebastian. I'm not even sure he knows more than what he has already told me. It is hard, up there in the sunlight, to believe that any ghosts or secrets could be chasing us. Surely Liesl and I, living amidst wealth in a great castle, protected by a powerful man, are safer than we have ever been or could ever hope to be again. What can I gain from learning what came before? We are in the "happily ever after" part of our fairy tale—or at least Liesl must be. She has her Bearskin.

Still, she does not seem quite as radiant as I had hoped she would be here, as mistress of her castle. She doles out only half-smiles, and her eyes have a far-off look to them. Perhaps it is only homesickness or the pressures of hosting all these events. When this garden is fin-ished, it shall be a wonderful surprise for her. If that is not enough, I will find something else to put her in good spirits again.

I shall bring Liesl's true smile back, whatever it takes.

CHAPTER TWENTY-THREE

Anne's Diary

2 OCTOBER

Something happened just now that has aroused my suspicion. Bluebeard joined us for tea in the library, and when he mistakenly took Liesl's teacup, Idonia quickly corrected him, assuring him that she had prepared his just as he likes it. He took the cup without making a fuss, and perhaps I am making too much of it, but when Idonia stopped him, her voice was edged with fear. I do not think I imagined it.

I have the most horrible thought, one which I cannot seem to shake. What if Liesl's low spirits are caused not by homesickness, but by an illness brought on by something Idonia has been giving her? Perhaps in her tea?

It seems too horrible to be true—like something out of one of my novels—but still, I worry. There must be some explanation for the changes in Liesl, and why else would Idonia be afraid that Bluebeard would take the wrong cup?

Too long have I stalled on my investigations, content to grow flowers and laugh in the sunshine with Sebastian. That ends now. I will find out everything I can about Idonia, starting with her garden. I managed to find a book in the library that should help me identify the plants within it, and I shall sneak down there with my lantern after she goes to bed tonight.

Oh Liesl, how could I let you down like this? I have neglected you and let you come to harm.

As I planned, I waited until all fell quiet in the castle, and I was sure Idonia and the other servants were fast asleep in their rooms on the topmost floor. Then I hugged the book close to me and took up a candlestick. The door to my room shut quietly behind me, and I hurried down the hallway, holding my breath as I passed Liesl's door.

The castle was different at this hour. Though everyone slept, there was an energy about it that was not there—or perhaps is only harder to notice—during the daytime. I felt as if I should meet someone around every corner, but I was alone.

As I passed the entrance to the tower that led beneath the castle, the one the fox had led me down, there was the unmistakable scent of roses again. Now that I have been working in the gardens, I realized that it wasn't the aroma of fresh roses but the earthier smell of cut roses wilting. It was so strong it made me pause and consider entering the tower and searching for its source. I stood in the hall, facing the shadowy doorway for far longer than I should have, before shaking my head. My aim was to find out about Idonia's garden, so I resolved to do that before investigating any other mysteries.

I continued to the grand staircase. Its silver-veined white marble looked wet as my candlelight spilled across it. The thin fabric of my nightdress floated behind me as I swept down the stairs. I'd considered wearing my gardening dress for this endeavor, but if anyone caught me, it would be easier to pretend I'd been sleepwalking or grown confused by dreams or nightmares if I was still wearing sleeping clothes.

The ornate front door was heavy, but I managed to pull it open without making too much noise, and slipped outside into the moonlight. I blew out my candle and made my way through the gardens, wishing I had thought to hide my cloak somewhere outside. The chill raised bumps on my arms, and I knew that if anyone were awake and looked out one of the castle windows, my white nightdress would stand out against the dark landscape.

I should have been afraid, but at this point in my nighttime venture, I was not. I felt exhilarated to see the quiet calm of midnight. Many of the flowers were furled, waiting to bloom again with the sun. This was the castle as it was not meant to be seen, and if I were mistress of it, I would consider taking nightly walks like this, when it would be all mine and not shared by the servants or other castle residents.

Of course, as I write, I remember what I was not thinking of then: that I *could* have been mistress of the castle, had I been brave enough to marry Bluebeard in Liesl's place. She might be safe at home now, perhaps even married to someone she could truly love.

I continued through the gardens until I reached the brick wall surrounding Idonia's plot. I jumped in fear at a noise behind me, but it was only an owl, hooting as it alighted from the garden wall. My blood raced then, and I looked around me. Though I felt as if I were being watched, I saw no one. Silly of me to be so spooked by a bird.

I hurried into Idonia's garden and let out a relieved breath when I saw she wasn't there. I did not realize until then that I'd had an irrational fear that she would be. But I'd seen her freely visit the garden so often during the day that she would have no reason to be there in the middle of the night.

I knelt by the foxgloves and thumbed through the book. The moon gave enough light for me to make out its beautiful illustrations and compare them with the flowers before me. I hoped I could identify them quickly and be safely back in my bed, but it took me some time before I found the first illustration that matched.

The unusual deep purple flowers I'd noted on my first visit to the gardens matched an illustration and description for wolf's bane. I gasped when I saw another name for the plant, the caption under the illustration showing the flower's strange, hooded shape: "Queen of Poisons." With growing anxiety, I remembered that though they are most often grown for their beauty, foxgloves, too, are poisonous.

Feeling sick, I thumbed through the book and matched others. The delicate white bells were lily of the valley. The pink starbursts on vibrant green bushes were oleander. The blue-and-yellow morning glories, too, were deadly. There was mountain laurel, larkspur, bloodroot. Poisons one and all.

I could not stop turning pages until I'd identified each plant, as if somehow the result would be different. When I got to the end, I dropped the book in the dirt and stared at nothing in horror.

Idonia was growing poisons in her private garden. Idonia made our afternoon tea every day, and, if she wanted to, could presumably slip something into every meal. My sister had been growing frail and troubled, but she did not know or would not tell me why. It was too terrible to be true, and yet, how else could all these pieces fit together?

Eventually, I came back to myself and realized the danger I would be in if Idonia found me there. I clasped the book to me again and brushed the dirt from my nightdress. As quickly and quietly as I could, I hurried back through the gardens. Before I reentered the castle, I saw a light in a window on the uppermost floor which had not been there when I came out.

Afraid I had been seen, I raced up the staircase and down the hall, shutting myself in my room. It was too great a risk, now, to enter the northwest tower and explore whatever lay below the castle that Idonia did not wish me to see. Perhaps another night, if I dared venture out again.

I leaned back against the door until my breathing calmed and I could hear that, aside from my heartbeat, all was silent and still.

Then I placed the candlestick back on my nightstand, hid the book under my pillow, and wept.

When my tears ran out, I relit the candle and wrote this. Now that I have calmed, I can see my best course of action. I must be vigilant about what Liesl consumes. I shall come up with some excuse to make afternoon tea for her and watch carefully at mealtimes. If she improves, I shall know what Idonia has done. Surely Bluebeard will not allow anyone to poison his young bride, and when I reveal what I know, he shall be rid of her, and we can be at peace again. Liesl will be safe, healthy, and happy, as I have tried to keep her all along.

I must not tell her, though. I must tell no one until I am sure of what I suspect.

Never have I felt like this before. How strange it is to have gone from a house bursting at the seams with family and a whole herd of goats and flock of chickens, and here I am, alone. I wish I could tell Sebastian or Cristina, or even Bluebeard. But after discovering Idonia's poison garden, I see this castle has more secrets than I thought, and I can trust no one.

CHAPTER TWENTY-FOUR

Bluebeard's Diary | Thekla

14 NOVEMBER, 5TH YEAR OF QUEEN THERESA I

I did not mean to fall again, but I think even a greater man than I would have been powerless against Thekla's charms. Her easy laugh, her whimsical love of woodland walks . . . it was hard to tell how much was truly her and how much was an enchanting mask she wielded like a weapon. She broke at least a dozen hearts of my acquaintance before I met her myself, and she promptly left her other suitors behind.

We first encountered each other at one of my balls, and though she hid it well, I saw that she was impressed by my home and by the sheer decadence I put on display.

She approached me, all tanned skin and wicked, sparkling green eyes, and the next thing I knew, I had her in my arms, moving with her, feeling her warmth as we spun across the dance floor.

Our courtship was brief and seemed almost unnecessary. We both knew what we wanted, and what we were getting. Her, my name and wealth and status. Me, her beauty and charm, to display as the crown jewels of my opulent estate. We both realized and respected that we would never have each other's hearts. I did not want it, anyway. But I did need her obedience, and I suspected that would be nearly as hard to win.

Over the years, I have implemented a few changes to hide my secret. No servant stays longer than a decade, and I have a reputation for rotating through my acquaintances, cutting old friendships off at random while initiating contact with new nobles on a whim. It grows tiring, I admit, but it is necessary. I cannot have anyone around long enough to notice that I am never sick, that I do not age.

This, of course, is not so easy to manage with a wife. But Thekla seemed so little interested in *me* that I thought there was a chance. I even believed that, should she learn my secret, she might succeed where Cacilie had failed and be persuaded to join me. After all, her sharp, mercenary spirit was one of the things I admired most about her.

Alas, it was not to be. When I returned home today, Thekla awaited me on the marble stair, a gleaming dagger in her hand. She tossed her wavy dark hair over her shoulder and said, in a voice that trembled with both fear and rage, "Explain yourself."

My heart swelled in my chest. She was a fighter. She could under-stand my need to live and keep on living, to risk everything and pay any price to escape the shadows of death and decay.

So I explained. Calmly, pragmatically. I saw her trying to hide it, but she, too, was horrified by me.

"You and I are the same," I said. "Do you not see? You are willing to do whatever it takes to survive. So am I. And we can continue like that, forever." I reached my hand out to her. "Spend eternity at my side, Thekla."

"Do not touch me," she said, each word sharp and staccato. "You will never touch me again."

I began again. To explain, to entreat, to convince.

But she had heard enough. While I was still speaking, she spat, "I'll never join you, and I will not be next." Then she plunged the dagger into my heart.

I smiled sadly, pulled the dagger from my chest and threw it aside. Thekla did not bother to hide the terror and disgusted wonder in her eyes then. She knew there was no point; that it was too late for her.

CHAPTER TWENTY-FIVE

Anne's Diary

3 OCTOBER

All day I have felt quite sick. Sebastian noticed and sent me inside after a few hours, promising that he would save the last bits of the garden until tomorrow so we could finish it together. I spent the rest of the day pacing the Great Gallery or "helping" in the kitchens—where I learned Idonia rarely dwells and so probably never tampers with anyone's food—until it was nearly teatime.

I wandered down to the kitchens again, trying to seem as if it was almost a coincidence, and steeled myself to face Idonia.

She was puttering over the tray with its three lovely teacups, filling the cream and sugar containers, and brewing tea. Her black hair with its white streak was in a perfect knot, as usual, and her wrinkled hands were steady and sure as she performed the movements.

"Hello, Idonia," I said.

She looked up and blinked in surprise, but did not seem disturbed. "Good afternoon, Fraulein Anne."

"I wondered," I said, licking my lips nervously. I had planned to make it sound like the impulse of a moment, or something I had just thought of, but was failing miserably. I clasped my hands behind my back so she could not see them shake. "I wondered if I might prepare the tea for my sister."

She arched an eyebrow. "If my methods of preparation are not to your liking, you have only to tell me, and I shall change."

"It is not that," I said. "It is only . . . well, you must have noticed her spirits have been rather low lately." I smiled warmly, and she seemed to soften in response.

"I have noticed."

"I thought that perhaps if I made the tea as we used to, the familiarity might help her. She has been rather homesick."

"Make it however you like," she said as she arranged a pile of little cakes on a plate. "But hurry. The master will not like taking his tea late."

I tried to discern if this upset her at all, but it did not seem to. She even left the kitchen for a few minutes as I put the kettle on, and I switched Liesl's and my teacups out for fresh ones from the cupboard, just in case. Bluebeard's was the same size as ours and had the same pattern, but with black roses instead of red.

The water boiled, and I finished the tea, adding the amount of cream I knew Liesl liked. Idonia carried the tea tray up to the library again, but Bluebeard was not there, so after we took our cups and cakes from the tray, she went to find him.

She didn't seem at all bothered by me making the tea, so I had to wonder if I'd imagined it all. Perhaps I read too many novels, to be imagining housekeepers poisoning young brides. What would she gain, anyway, if Liesl died? I do not think we trouble her greatly enough for her to wish us gone. Several of the servants had even told me that the castle felt much more alive now that we had come.

"The tea tastes different than usual," Liesl remarked, then took another long sip.

A bead of sweat rolled from my hairline and into the collar of my dress. Was the taste different only because I had made it, or because it was lacking whatever Idonia usually laced it with?

Forcing my voice to steady, I said, "That's because I made it. I thought it might be nice to have a taste of home."

"It is like home, but better," she said and smiled. I supposed the tea leaves were of better quality than we were ever able to buy before. "You must make the tea every day now. Or show Idonia how."

"Of course, if you wish," I said, breathing in the fragrant steam from my own teacup to steady myself. This was just what I wanted, but now I felt sillier than ever. I was far too old to be indulging in these flights of fancy, suspecting such horrible things of old house-keepers.

There's no doubt that she is growing poisons in her garden, but perhaps she only uses them for rats or other pests. Perhaps she does not use them at all—many are as beautiful as they are deadly.

I had quite resolved to put these suspicions behind me, and I nearly have, except for one thing. Before dinner, I took the flower guidebook from under my pillow so I could return it to its proper shelf in the library. Liesl was in the library, though, so I sat for a few minutes and casually perused the book so she would not think I was hiding it from her. She often asks about the books I read as she embroiders, though today she was in better spirits than usual and singing softly to herself as she worked.

The book fell open in my lap to one of the front pages, and I saw that it had been inscribed. It read, "To my darling Rosalind, with love from your new husband, Bluebeard." It was dated as well—from nearly thirty-five years ago.

I stared at it for a long time, wanting to be sure my eyes did not deceive me. The fox and fireflies I could have imagined, but those words were there in solid black ink. After flipping through the pages and finding no other annotations, I slipped it back into the bookcase with trembling hands and retired early to my room so I might write this.

How can this be? Bluebeard is at most forty-five years old himself, and yet he wrote to a wife that long ago? Was his father also known as Bluebeard? Somehow that seems unlikely. I wish I had a sample of Bluebeard's handwriting with which to compare, but I cannot very well ask Liesl for one. If I put the date aside, I see what this shows: he has had another wife besides Liesl and Amalie. And if there have been two before my sister, how many more might there have been? The village rumors dared to guess as high as seven.

I must get to the bottom of this. I shall write to Klaus and see if he has heard anything more. I wish I had thought to look through the other books in the library, but it is too late to do so now. Tomorrow. And I shall keep this diary on my person from now on. Who knows what might befall me if either Bluebeard or Idonia—or anyone else in this household with something to hide—should see that I am close to uncovering their secrets?

Chapter Twenty-Six

Letter from Anne

3 October

Dearest Klaus,

As always, I hope this letter finds you and all our family well. Liesl and I are quite well too, though we miss you all keenly. There is comfort in familiarity, and we have so little of that here. It really feels a different world than the one we knew before.

The sheen and excitement of attending balls and dinners has worn off somewhat, and I now find myself thinking often of home. Has Ritter whittled any new creatures lately? He was working on a hedgehog when we left home. How is Heller's business coming along?

And oh, how excited we are at Warner and Silvia's news! I do wish I could be with her now, so be sure Warner and the rest of you provide whatever help she requires. Liesl and I are both so excited that we shall be aunts! We have taken bets already on the baby. Liesl fiercely believes we'll be blessed with a nephew, but I think we already have quite enough men in our family and that Silvia would love having a daughter.

It is funny that I should be missing home now. I never liked autumn so much at home—everything is dying and dull, and there is not the sense of coziness that comes with winter. I hope the harvest has gone well for our neighbors, and that Frau Frida has not been cheating you when you sell her our goat milk. I was always the one who could extract the best prices from her, but I suppose that job has fallen to you now, Klaus. I shall give you some advice: ask her of her grandchildren when you first arrive, and she will be much kinder when you get down to bargaining.

Since my last letter, I have taken on a new project. There is a neglected garden here, filled with beautiful black flowers, and I have decided to restore it. I have spent the last week working it with the gardener, and it has felt so refreshing to work the soil—to work at all, really. It is too late in the year to see its full glory, no matter how we toil, but come spring, I think it will be a marvel. I imagine whoever first planted it would be pleased to know it shall bring joy to people once again.

There is one last thing, Klaus, and I am afraid I cannot speak plainly of it. Remember the rumors you told me of before we left? I have tried to seek out the truth of them, but I am no closer than when we arrived. If you have found out anything more, please send word. Ask Silvia, too. She may have heard something in the village.

Oh, how we miss you all. I have not yet spoken to Liesl or Blue-beard of a Christmas visit, but I really begin to think it a necessity. Perhaps you could stay for a week or more, and we could have as merry a time as we did leading up to the wedding. If I can arrange it, do promise you shall all come.

With all Liesl's and my love,

Anne

CHAPTER TWENTY-SEVEN

Anne's Diary

4 OCTOBER

It is early morning, and no one else is yet awake, but I have already searched through the library. Late last night, I had the idea to look for more inscriptions in books. I had found Rosalind's name that way; might there be others? After pulling every book off the shelf, all I found were a dozen books inscribed with book plates reading "Ex Libris: Margaret." The ink was faded, so I do not know how long ago it was that Margaret claimed these books, but I have a horrible, dreadful feeling that she, too, had once been Bluebeard's wife.

I must go now, but I wanted to write all this down so that I will not doubt myself later.

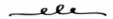

Sebastian and I finished restoring the garden today. I was not in my customary good mood, and I think he could tell. He was merrier than usual and tried to make me smile with his little jokes and teasing. The garden on the hill is beautiful now. The black roses and pansies and hollyhocks have been revealed, the debris and weeds cleared away. Not all the flowers are black, it turns out. Many are edged in red or deep purple or other dark colors. All of them are wonderful.

The stone path up the hill is cleared now, too, as are the stepping stones that wind through the garden. We left some of the ivy along the walls and gates—just enough to give it a hint of the forgotten look that it had when I first discovered it. The last thing we cleared were the vines that had grown up around the stone fountain at the center of the garden. The water in it does not flow anymore, but I plan to ask Bluebeard to have it repaired come spring.

Though I cannot wait to show the garden to Liesl, I appreciated having one last day in it with only Sebastian. The place is perhaps only known to the two of us still, as Idonia has never asked me about our progress. We have worked hard to make it as beautiful as it must have been when it was first created. Often, as I dug up weeds by the roots or trimmed back vines, I wondered who might have dreamt up this place and then worked to make it real.

I do not think it was Bluebeard, and I have a feeling it was Rosalind. She must have loved plants and flowers for Bluebeard to have given her the book. I wish I could ask someone, but I do not dare. Not even Sebastian, though I long to tell him.

Heady floral scents tickled my nose as we wandered the meandering stone path through the garden, but I quickly grew accustomed to them. When we finally stopped at the fountain, Sebastian said something unusual.

He half-smiled and said, "Thank you for your help, Anne. I've wanted to restore this garden for quite some time, but I needed permission. I am not sure I could have finished it by winter without your assistance, and I am glad you were able to put your mark on this place before you leave."

I'd started to blush at his first words, but then I looked at him in confusion. "Before I leave?"

"Yes," he said, holding my gaze. More softly, he said, "I knew you would not stay forever, and there are reasons I am glad you will not be. But I shall miss you."

I frowned. "I'm not sure what you've heard, but I have no plans to leave at present."

"You don't?" It was his turn to look perplexed and a little embarrassed.

"No," I said. "And I would like to know who has said as much." Could it have been Liesl? Was she planning to send me back home?

Sebastian rubbed the back of his neck. "It was only . . . some of the servants were talking. They thought a proposal might be coming your way soon." He coughed awkwardly. "Perhaps several, they said."

My cheeks heated, and I looked away. The next ball is tomorrow night, and I had given no thought to Franz or Gustav in days. My worries about Idonia and Liesl had kept me busy, but if I was honest with myself, Sebastian had occupied my thoughts as well. More than any of my suitors had.

"The other servants have been misinformed," I said as coolly as I could. "Someday, I suppose I shall—" I stopped, uncomfortable with saying anything further in front of Sebastian. If we had met when my sister and I were only goatherds, how different things would be! But I knew how much Liesl desired that I make a good match now. I shook my head to clear my thoughts. "My sister needs me."

He nodded. It wounded my pride a little that he did not seem happier about me staying, or hearing that I had no plans of matrimony yet. In fact, he pressed his lips together and glanced back at the castle. Still not looking at me, he said, "I hear Bluebeard means to go away soon."

He had said as much this morning at breakfast. "I believe he does, but only for a fortnight."

"Perhaps you and Liesl should return home for the duration of his absence," Sebastian said. "After he leaves, you could go, and come back just before he returns."

"Why would we do that?" This was our home now; couldn't Sebastian see that? Surely in all our conversations, he'd seen how hard I was working to make it so. To fit here.

He turned back to me and studied my face for a few long moments, weighing his words. "It would be safer."

"Are we back to this? You cannot tell me there is danger and then refuse to explain your warnings. Nothing has happened, and I feel perfectly safe." The last two things were untruths. A few things had happened: I'd followed a fox beneath the castle and been scolded away, discovered the poison garden, and learned of Amalie and Rosalind and Margaret. But even taken all together, they didn't seem like much more than "nothing."

"I wish . . ." Sebastian looked down at his hands. "I wish you could always feel so. If there were anything I could do, I—but I worry that things may happen when the master leaves. Things that have happened before."

"I shall not listen to cryptic warnings any longer. If you can't explain, then I must assume the danger is not real." I leaned against the fountain and put one hand on my hip. "Besides, you'll be here. That's something, isn't it?"

He shook his head, and my heart sank. If he didn't want to protect us from these imagined dangers, why was he even telling me of them? But he'd shaken his head for a slightly different reason. "I won't be here when he goes. I leave the same day."

"You're going with him?"

"No," Sebastian said. "He is sending me to an auction so I can purchase more rare tulip bulbs for the south garden. It just happens to coincide with his departure."

"How long will you be gone?"

"At least a week, maybe longer."

"And why do you think we'll be in danger? Is it Idonia?" I asked before I could check my tongue.

"Idonia?" His brow furrowed. "Why would you think that?"

I bit my lip, failing to not look guilty. "Well, if you and Bluebeard are gone, who else is left to put us in danger?"

He shook his head and grimaced. "This is not a joke to me, Anne. If I knew more, I would tell you. If the things I do know were not so dangerous to tell... Anyway, I have proof of nothing, but I worry."

Sebastian was really distressed then, and it was hard to see him like that. "We'll be cautious," I said. "You do not need to worry for us."

He stared at the castle again and said, "I hope all will be well."

A charged silence stretched between us. He wanted to say more, I could tell. I wanted to say something, but the things I truly wanted to tell him were far too mortifying to form into words, and the witty things I hoped to say instead would not come.

Finally, Sebastian gripped the edge of the fountain and let out a long breath. "Anne?" he asked softly. "What is it that you want?"

The truth, I thought right away. *Safety for my sister*. I wanted to know everything about this place—all its secrets and mysteries. But that was not an answer likely to calm him.

"I want what everyone wants," I said instead. "A good, happy life. For my family and friends to be safe and healthy." And they are not lies, exactly. Isn't that what Liesl wanted, too, and why she and I had come here in the first place?

He gave me another long, hard look, and this time it was so intense that I had to look away. "If that's what you want," he said in a resigned way, "then you need to stop looking into the past. Be content with the joys of the present. Please. For both your sake and your sister's."

Sebastian's words seemed so earnest that I found myself agreeing, then feeling a stab of guilt for lying to him. He couldn't be correct; how could ignoring the past and the fates of the other wives—however many there may have been—help Liesl?

He seemed greatly relieved by my false promise, and I thought a subject change was best. "Please," I said, "I do not wish to end today like this. Can we take one more turn about the garden and enjoy our hard work?"

Slowly, he pulled his gaze away from the castle down below. Then he offered me his arm. "Of course."

These last days, working in the garden with him, have been my happiest since we came here. To have a purpose besides worrying for Liesl was wonderful, and his company and conversation were easy in a way that not even Liesl's are anymore. Though I am proud of our work, I am melancholy and listless to see it end.

But I did not focus on these things then. Instead, I tried to do as he said, and focus on present joys. The feel of his arm, the fragrant flowers, the castle glowing in the sunlight, and Sebastian's slow pace, as if he, too, wished to stretch long our last little stroll in our beautiful garden.

Chapter Twenty-Eight

Anne's Diary

5 October

Well, I have just come from talking with Liesl, and it sounds as if this shall be the last ball for some time, and not just because Bluebeard leaves in a few days. She was so busy with preparations for his journey that I was not even able to show her the garden on the hill today. I suppose it will have to wait until tomorrow, if she is not too tired from the ball.

The evening started well, or as well as it could have for two girls weary of festivities and rich food and late nights spent dancing. If we could somehow show ourselves, back in the meadow just before we met Bluebeard, our future spent in finery and merriment, I imagine those girls would be disappointed in us growing tired of it all so very soon.

Which is not to say I had no enjoyment in it. It was a masquerade ball, so everyone put extra effort into their costumes for the evening, using the occasion as an excuse to trim every possible surface in gold and lace, to wear the finest satins and silks. Cristina found me a white mask of pearls and lace and feathers, and it went quite well with my dress. I looked rather like a swan, though I'm sure I was not half so graceful.

There was also good food and drink, and my two suitors to see. I first danced a polka with good-spirited Gustav, then a Ländler with the regal Franz, and so on for two hours, changing between them every few dances. I didn't feel much like talking, but it didn't seem to matter to either of them. My smiles were enough for Gustav, and Franz took advantage of my reticence to lead me through many perfectly executed spins and twirls and dips. He really is an excellent dancer.

The trouble began when I excused myself to the balcony for some fresh air. A figure dressed all in black leaned back against the wrought-iron rail, watching the dancing through the glass doors. The muffled melody of a waltz made it through, but all else was quiet and still on the broad stone landing overlooking the gardens. A great many stars were visible, but my eyes were drawn to the stranger. He wore a mask over his eyes, black trimmed with silver, but there was something familiar about his lanky form.

"Sebastian?"

He finally looked at me, though I'd gotten the sense that he had seen me come out and knew I was there. "Anne," he said shortly, bowing.

"What are you doing out here?"

"Where else would I be, but in the gardens where I work?"

"Yes, but you're . . . " I indicated his outfit. "You look rather dashing. I can't imagine you were gardening in this." The other servants wore masks tonight, too, but I hadn't expected to see him.

"I don't make a habit of it," he said, his face still serious. "But I thought to bring you this." He pulled out a black rose—which could only have been from our garden—and slipped it behind my ear. I smiled and blushed, but he turned away.

"You must come in and dance with me," I said.

"I do not think you shall have the time."

"What?"

"You have no lack of partners."

"Well, I *am* an excellent dancer," I said lightly, laughing a little.

He smiled thinly. "I noticed."

"You must dance with me to make things even," I said. "Since you know how well I dance, but I have no idea of your skill."

"I cannot go in there."

I shrugged. "We could dance here, then."

Sebastian looked out over the gardens and let out a slow breath, visible in the chill night air. I worried I had been too forward and was about to claim it only a joke, when he turned back to me and said, "I suppose I could, this once."

The band struck up another lovely waltz then, and it was settled. I held my hand out to him. He took it more gently than I expected and placed his hand on my waist, barely touching me, as if he were afraid I might break. We stepped off and let the music take us.

It was strange to be so close to him. I had been even closer, of course, a few times in the garden and during the riding lesson. But this was different. I could feel the hard muscles of his shoulder and the strength of his hand through my gloves, though he held me so delicately. He smelled like something warm and earthy, and our breaths, clouding in the cool air, mingled together.

We did not speak, but we met each other's gaze in the moonlight. His eyes had always looked gray from a distance, but after seeing them so close, I discerned that they were a soft blue. I also noticed the freckle on his temple and the small scar above his eyebrow. I wondered if he was finding anything new in my face.

When the song ended, we did not pull apart right away. Our eyes were still locked, his lips parted ever so slightly, and for a mad moment, I wanted to kiss him. Instead, I cleared my throat and said, "Well, you dance quite well after all." My voice came out high and thin, but he didn't seem to notice. His fiery eyes were still locked on mine.

"I wish . . . " he said softly, in a tone that said it was too late for whatever he wished.

The tension was too much, and I stepped to the balcony rail again. I turned my head toward the star-strewn sky, so I would not have to look at him or the flowers he so carefully tended. He joined me, and when the silence between us stretched too long, I said softly, "What is it you wish?" In a lighter tone, I added, "Perhaps we shall see a falling star, and you may wish upon it."

He shook his head, the corners of his mouth turned down. "I wish I did not have to go."

"You shall only be gone for a week," I said. "Or has that changed?"

"Much can happen in a week," he said darkly. Then he turned to me and took one of my satin-gloved hands in his. "These last few weeks, working with you in the garden . . . It has been wonderful."

My eyes lowered to my shoes. "For me as well, Sebastian."

"I have begun to . . . worry for you. If only there were some way to know you shall be safe while I am away." He dropped my hand, and his own clenched into a fist.

For a moment, I thought he had been about to express something more. That he had grown to care for me, perhaps. But what a silly thought that was. He was only continuing, as always, to warn me of dangers he could not describe. "I'm sure I shall be quite alright."

"Please, Anne," he said, leaning close enough that I could breathe in his now-familiar scent again. "Believe me when I say you must be cautious. Do not go looking into the past as you have done before."

"Why should I believe you? You've kept secrets from me."

"I have told you all that I know that is safe to tell—"

"Truly? Then who is Margaret?"

His eyebrows pulled together in confusion. I wanted to believe the expression was sincere—that he didn't know anything about whatever horrible fate befell the other wives. But there were too many lies and secrets and hidden things here, and I didn't know whom to trust: Bluebeard, Idonia, Sebastian? Even Liesl, I suspected, knew more than she had told me.

"I've never heard that name before," Sebastian said carefully.

"But you can guess who it belonged to?"

He swallowed, nodded. "I can guess."

Another dance ended, and all we could hear were the muffled murmurs that made it through the glass and the chirping of the night insects.

"Do you still think I should go?" I said, hating the strain in my voice from my suddenly parched throat. "Is there no reason for me to stay?"

"It isn't safe here for you. Please, if you have a chance to be free of this place, take it."

My eyes stung with withheld tears. "What about Liesl?"

He shook his head. "It's too late for her. It was over for her the day she married him."

I felt as if he had slapped me. All I wanted was to keep Liesl safe, and now he was telling me I had already failed?

"How can you say that? I would do anything for my sister. If it's too late for her, it's too late for me."

He let out a frustrated huff and ran his hands through his hair. "You must see that, as his wife, she is tied to the castle now in ways you are not. But you—you have a chance to escape this place." He gave a pained glance back through the ballroom windows and muttered, "Several chances, by the looks of it."

"What do you mean?" I asked, throwing my hands in the air. "You tell me how you have enjoyed my company these past weeks, and I also had begun to feel—" I shook my head and took a deep breath, clinging to anger. "Now you push me away, into the arms of my other would-be suitors?" It took me a moment to realize what I'd said—that I'd implied Sebastian was another of my suitors—and my cheeks burned.

"It's better if you're safe, far from here," he said, not looking at me. Then he exhaled heavily, and it hung in the air over the balcony. "Besides, it could never have worked between us."

My heart felt as if someone were squeezing it. My eyes pricked with tears. I had not even realized until that moment that I had imagined a future for us together—at the very least, both still living at the castle and gardening and speaking to each other every day—and it had already been torn from me.

"If—" I said, but it came out with an embarrassing tremble. I cleared my throat and tried again. "If that is how you feel, then I do not know why I am out here with you. Good night."

With as much dignity as I could muster, I swept up my skirts and made for the ballroom. His hand caught mine once again, but I yanked it away from him.

"I'm sorry," he said. "But I believe it's for the best. If you have any affection for me, give it to one of your other suitors, for it is wasted on me. Leave this castle while you still can."

I fled to the ballroom without another glance back at him. At the door, I remembered the rose behind my ear and dropped it behind me. Inside, I stumbled into Gustav but brushed past him until I found Liesl, sitting demurely next to Bluebeard as he regaled his guests with a tale of his hunting prowess. Upon seeing my face, Liesl excused herself and pulled me into an arched nook off the ballroom so we could talk privately.

"What is it?" she asked, gently brushing back a strand of hair that had come loose from my updo.

I realized my mistake. I had run to my sister for comfort instinctively, but I could not tell her the details of what had upset me. "I spoke with Sebastian, and he said some things that upset me."

"The gardener?" she asked, her eyebrows pulling together. I only nodded. "I see. Well, I don't know why he is at the ball, but do you think you can go and dance with Herr Gustav or Herr Franz in good spirits, or shall I make excuses for you so that you can retire early?"

"I wish to retire early," I said. "If it will not trouble you too much to manage hostess duties on your own."

"Of course not."

"Oh, why must we have balls and such at all?" I asked. Even dancing with Franz or laughing with Gustav no longer appealed to me, now that I saw the future I longed for was not with either of them. And even if it were, how could I leave Liesl when she was so ill? The glow from the chandeliers was not enough to warm her pallor; they only showed the deep circles beneath her eyes all the more.

"I have been thinking the same," she said. "I have talked to Bluebeard, and now that all of his acquaintances have met me, he does not care how often I host such events. Perhaps a break is in order."

"You would do that for me?" I wiped away a pesky tear that had started to run down my cheek.

"Of course," she said, with so much warmth in her gaze that I almost began to cry again. "Though truth be told, I am growing weary of them too. It is so much planning and work for little enjoyment on my part. Bluebeard does not dance, and I should feel it wrong to stand up with another."

I kissed her good night and returned to my quarters. At the time, I was too upset over Sebastian to notice it, but now I feel great guilt that all along I had been enjoying these events which so taxed my sister. I tried to sleep but found myself too agitated, so I got up and wrote all this. It is nearly dawn now, and my eyelids are heavy with sleep. At least now, with no more balls, I shall get long nights of sleep again.

Sebastian leaves tomorrow, and I have vowed to think of him no more.

CHAPTER TWENTY-NINE

Bluebeard's Diary | Liesl

5 OCTOBER, 24TH YEAR OF KING LUKAS IV

I am most pleased with my bride.

She looks quite as well as I expected now that she is dressed and styled in the latest fashions. I see the way the other lords envy my good fortune, and it pleases me. I did not believe she would truly become the mistress of the castle and hostess of my parties. I had rather expected to leave those tasks to Idonia, but she has taken on the challenge and done well. She is young and lively and so much of her life is ahead of her, for me to enjoy.

Her sister, I worried, might cause me trouble, as she seems of an inquisitive turn of mind. But with the way she is courting young noblemen, I suppose she shall not be here much longer. Her influence on my bride will enhance my test of her loyalty. If my bride can stymie her curiosity, perhaps not even telling her sister of what I shall give her, that will be even further proof that she is the one.

It is rather a shame to test her at all. She is sweet, and even begins to seem as if she desires real affection to grow between us. I must remind myself that I have been here many times before. There was a page in the story of each love just like this—a page where I knew I had chosen well and found a companion who would obey me and stand beside me for her lifetime. They all failed me.

But perhaps this time shall be different. I leave tomorrow, and she shall be tested. If she is found lacking, she shall join the others. I can only wish she will succeed. After all, I would not have attempted this again had I not some small measure of hope.

CHAPTER THIRTY

Letter from Liesl

6 OCTOBER

Dearest Mother,

Bluebeard leaves today for a fortnight, and I am so happy I gathered the courage to have a real conversation with him first.

It all started at our last ball. Anne came to me upset and speaking of a disagreement with the gardener. I knew she had been working on a gardening project of late, but now I see why it made her so happy, why she hummed to herself as she chose books in the library and came in from outside every day tanned and sweating and smiling. She has formed an attachment with our young gardener.

I gave her leave to retire early from the ball and hoped that whatever had happened between them would be enough to sever the connection entirely. My first feeling was of anger and frustration—with all these events I've arranged, all these suitors I've helped coax her way, how can she spend all her time with a gardener? But then I examined these thoughts and found them rather cruel. After all, we were of the same station as the gardener only a few months ago, and Anne will be secure no matter what or who she chooses, thanks to my marriage. Why should I foist her on all these noble boys who, I see now, don't truly mean anything to her, when she might be happy with a servant? And she might stay here to both vex and comfort me in a way I would not trade for anything.

As my mind ran through these thoughts while sitting at the ball and half-listening to my husband and his friends, I realized that amidst my tangled emotions on the matter hid another, unsavory one: jealousy. I was envious of Anne, not just for her freedom to choose among all these suitors, but because she had managed to form a connection with the gardener in such a short time. Here I am, two months from first meeting my husband, and still I feel nothing for him.

Ah, what a dreadful thing that was to write. But the truth sometimes is dreadful.

He is kind and attentive enough to me when others are near, as he was last night at the ball, but when we are alone, I might as well be one of the furnishings. Something pleasant to look at, something that can be of use, but not something one grows to love. However, our conversation the other day gave me some small hope. When I asked to pause the events for a time, and he mentioned business taking him away from home for a fortnight, he was so amenable to all my suggestions that I really thought it best to just ask him for what I wanted.

I was tired after the ball, but I requested a word with my husband before we retired. The ball was a late one, for I find it is easier to avoid certain . . . unpleasant midnight occurrences if I'm awake and active and the castle is full of guests.

In any case, he obliged me, and we sat together in the library with warm cups of tea.

"My dear husband," I began, "I know you are leaving soon for a time, but I wanted to let you know that, when you return, I should like us to spend more time together."

"We see each other every day. I have not left the castle since you arrived."

"Yes, that is true." I agreed. "But we are so rarely alone, and when we are . . . well, we wed so quickly that there has not been much time to get to know one another. We are not able to converse freely and easily upon any subject, as I would wish."

He put his cup down then and looked at me, as if for the first time. I realized he hadn't really been listening until then. "You wish to know me better?"

"Well, yes. Of course I do. You're my husband; are we not to be partners in life?"

He took my hand then and pressed it, which he'd never done before. "You are a sweet little thing, aren't you?" he asked, as if to himself. "Yes, dear wife, if that is what you wish, then when I return—if all goes well in my absence—you shall have as much of my time and conversation as you could wish."

They were kinder words than he'd spoken since wooing me in Coesfeld, and I thought perhaps my heart should have done something—warmed or sped up or something of that sort—but I felt nothing.

I put on a smile anyway and said, "Thank you, my liege." Then, because it had gone so well, I decided to dare one more question. "You may have noticed I've not quite been at full health of late. I find it difficult to sleep in my room. There are strange things about and . . . well, I feel a bit silly asking this, but have you ever heard or seen or smelled strange things, at night in the castle? Things most . . . unnatural and unsettling."

I expected him to laugh at me, and indeed, a strange, knowing grin flashed across his face. But then it was gone, and his features returned to normal. "Oh, wife, all the excitement since you've arrived here must have addled your mind, and you are overtired from playing hostess. You mistake nightmares for what is real. Rest during my absence, and set your mind and health to rights once more. Speak no more of such nonsense."

"Yes. Of course, my dear husband. I must take better care of my health."

We retired for the evening then, and I felt hopeful that perhaps with more time and conversation together, I really shall grow to love and respect him as I should. Perhaps we only need more quiet moments together like this. And he must be right about my mind . . . I have feared as much. I hope that rest will do me good, and I can be in both better health and spirits when he returns.

Though, of course, I must also look out for Anne, after her little heartbreak at the ball. She has suggested we thoroughly explore every room of the castle while Bluebeard is gone. When we first arrived,

I enjoyed such games, but each day I grow weaker and I fear I also grow—now that I have spoken to my husband of it—more mad. But I shall play along to keep Anne's spirits up. That should not be too much for me.

I miss you more than words can say.

With all my love,

Liesl

CHAPTER THIRTY-ONE

Letter from Anne

6 OCTOBER

Dearest Klaus,

I'm delighted to hear that all is well with the family. Liesl is also quite happy to hear of home, though she is so preoccupied with her duties as lady of the castle that she hasn't found the time to write to you. The other night was our last ball for a while, however, so hopefully soon she will have time to write her own letters to you.

I am especially happy to hear that Silvia and our forthcoming niece or nephew are well. Thank you also for the update on little Sophie—you know how she's my favorite of this year's baby goats. Do you think that Ritter could sketch her for me, and that you could enclose the sketch with your next correspondence? It would bring me such happiness.

Perhaps it would bring cheer to Liesl, too. Bluebeard leaves the castle today and will not return for at least a fortnight. He has not said why he is going or to where, only that it's on business. Cristina, my maid, said the other servants told her he never goes away like this. The last time he left for several weeks, he came back with us.

At first, Liesl was unsettled by this bit of news, but she is content once again after I suggested that we spend the time exploring every inch of the castle. It is such a large estate, and there are so many rooms that we have yet to see.

This morning at breakfast, she told Bluebeard of our plan. He agreed that it was a fine idea and gave her the large brass circle of keys which he always wears at his side. "The castle is yours," he told us, smiling and stroking his long beard. "I hope you enjoy all of its treasures while I am away." After breakfast, he whispered something to Liesl about the keys—perhaps he was suggesting where we should start our journey.

I feel foolish, but I am full of a sort of girlish excitement at this little adventure. As a child, I always dreamt of moving to a far-off land and exploring magnificent dwellings full of riches, just like the heroes of our favorite tales. The parts of the castle which we have already explored have been so splendid, I know there must be more wonderful sights to behold. I only wish I had some small amount of Ritter's ability to capture a scene in charcoal or paint. Then I could show you the things I love here.

But perhaps you shall be seeing them yourself soon. Have you talked to Father about visiting? December grows closer every day, and I long to see you and our other brothers! It would bring Liesl and me such joy.

Please send our best wishes to everyone. I hope to see you soon.

Your loving sister,

Anne

Chapter Thirty-Two

Anne's Diary

9 October

I have not written here in days, and I shall not write any further of Sebastian or my conversation with him at the ball. I have spent enough time sulking about it that it's no use to describe it here, too.

It could never have worked between us. How many times those words have run through my mind! I shall go mad.

Anyway, he's gone. I was tempted to see him off, to try to repair things between us, but he left so early the morning after the ball that I did not get the chance. Though, when I left my chambers, I found a black rose outside the door. Perhaps it was meant as an apology. I ripped its petals off one by one and threw them out the window, watching them float away, black teardrops on the wind. I shall endeavor to think of him no more.

Bluebeard left shortly after breakfast the same day. Sadly, Liesl has been too weary to explore the castle with the keys he gave us before he set off. She is so weak that I have not thought it wise to venture out to the garden on the hill, either, though I dearly wish to show it to her. Of course, that garden has other, painful associations for me now.

I had a letter from Klaus this morning. He knows nothing more about Bluebeard's past than he did at the wedding—it seems the village gossips have moved on. Perhaps they have all but forgotten the two of us who used to live among them. It saddens me a little. If any of the other girls had married a nobleman, I don't think I would ever cease to think of them. But perhaps those thoughts would be bitter and envy-laced, so it may be for the best. Though, it does not help my worries over Liesl.

Each day since Bluebeard left, she has grown increasingly pale, and the shadows beneath her eyes deepen with every night that passes. Idonia's behavior is unaltered, and I continue to make her tea, so I still don't know what ails her. I even once considered that her wedding ring could somehow be draining her strength. Clearly, I read far too many novels.

I do know that she has not been sleeping properly, for the servants tell me she spends the evenings pacing her room and wringing her hands. I have tried to entice her with a walk in the closest gardens, a lovely book from the library, or a new dish that Cook has dreamt up for her, but to no avail. Liesl has withdrawn into herself, to somewhere I cannot reach.

Despite their whispers, and though we have been here such a short time, the servants are all quite devoted to Liesl. They do their part to ensure that the furnishings are without dust, the windows clean and cheery, and the hearth fires blazing. They also smile whenever they see her. I hear them whisper between themselves, "the poor little thing," and "such a shame, she is so pleasant, but it cannot last." There is such pity in their voices that my heart aches. I remember what Cook said about their superstitions, and I worry.

I wish I knew what distresses her, but she tells me nothing.

I tried, once again, to ask her this morning in the library. Since she was not forthcoming on her own, I tried to make guesses.

"Does he . . . treat you well?" I asked delicately.

Liesl's face went carefully blank. "He is gentle with me; do not worry yourself on that account."

I pursed my lips. Something was wrong. But we were treading too close to improper subjects. I disliked it; never before had there been secrets between us. And now, when it was perhaps most important that there were none, a large part of her life has become something I cannot yet know.

"If there is anything wrong, you can tell me. Please. I want to help."

Liesl stood and walked to the window, looking down at the gardens through the colored glass. She placed a hand on the windowsill to support herself and let out a world-weary sigh. "There is much you do not understand, Anne. I hope you never will."

"What do you mean?" I asked, upset at the patronizing way she spoke. "Liesl, please, I can see you are not well. Just tell me why. Is it Bluebeard?"

"I married him, didn't I?" she snapped. "I knew what I was doing."

I blinked in surprise, not knowing how to connect what she said to our conversation. Before I could ask again, she dismissed me, saying she wanted to be left alone. With a heavy heart, I left the library.

The first day, I thought Liesl was only longing for Bluebeard's company, but now I can't guess what is upsetting her. Between her pallor and the servants' whisperings, I imagine the ghastliest things. With the rumors of Bluebeard's previous wives, I wonder if there is not some evil in this castle. Perhaps the servants are right about a curse, and something is haunting her. I am resolved to find out what it is. At dinner tonight, I will plead that she reveals what has been plaguing her. If I cannot help her, I fear the worst.

Liesl has revealed to me the cause of her distress, and I feel foolish at my wild imaginings from before; there are no ghosts or evil spirits here. This is but a castle—though extravagant, it is a home the same as any other.

But I am running ahead of myself. I shall write down what came to pass at our dinner this evening.

Cook, kind woman that she is, created an extravagant menu in the hopes of improving Liesl's spirits. The first course passed slowly and with little conversation. Liesl would barely touch her creamy potato soup. My stomach was unsettled as I noticed how pale and thin she has grown, a stark contrast from even last week. Dark circles ring her eyes, and her eyelids seem heavy, as if she has not slept in quite some time.

During the next course, which was an equally delightful dish of roasted quail with asparagus, I mustered up the courage to beg her again to tell me what is making her ill. I even hinted, as delicately as I could, that perhaps I should suspect another niece or nephew to follow soon after Warner and Silvia's child. She looked at me carefully, as if she hadn't truly seen me in days. Then she dismissed the servants from the room, and I knew she was going to confess all to me.

"It is nothing like you suggest," she said as she sighed and took my hands in hers. "My dearest Anne." Her dark-stoned wedding ring once fit snugly, but it spun loose on her finger now that she had grown weaker.

"Yes?" I replied.

"You recall the morning Bluebeard left, when we talked of our plans to explore the castle?"

I nodded. So she did remember. I tried to hide how sorely disappointed I was by our canceled adventure.

"Well," she continued, "Bluebeard pulled me aside after breakfast in order to give me the keys to the castle."

"Of course, Liesl, you must remember, I was there—"

She gave me a stern look, the way she always did when I grew more impatient than a lady should be. Usually, that look annoyed me, but I was glad to see this spark of the old Liesl.

"Yes, but afterward, he pulled me aside," she said, "and gave me another key." She unfurled her left palm and extended it toward me. Inside was a golden key. She had held it so tightly and for so long that the outline of the little key was imprinted on her palm.

Something held me back from touching the key with my own hand. "But Liesl, why would this key cause you such distress?"

She clasped the key into her fist again and put her hand back at her side. "Because he told me that we may explore every inch of this castle except for the room that this key unlocks."

My meal was left untouched on my plate as I contemplated this. "That is strange, but why does it upset you so?"

"I do not know. It haunts me. What could be in that room? Why shouldn't I look inside it? And, if he did not wish me to see its contents, why entrust me with the key?"

"Curiosity is a heavy burden to bear," I said, thinking of all I had not told her. Of Amalie and Rosalind and Margaret. Of poison gardens and obscure warnings. I moved a curl that had fallen from her updo behind her ear and smiled.

"It has helped to tell you. But still, it weighs on me."

"There is just one thing for it then—we shall have to find out for ourselves!" I said eagerly. She wasn't the only one bearing unanswered questions.

She gasped. "No, Anne, we mustn't. The way he spoke to me when he warned me not to use this key made a shiver run through my whole body. I am too frightened to disobey him." She ran her hands over her cheeks, covering her eyes. "I cannot."

"Very well," I said, embracing her. "We shan't look if you do not wish it."

She nodded into my shoulder. The windows had darkened outside, and the candlelight basked us in a golden glow.

"Do you know which room the key is for?" I asked, though something in me already knew it was the room beneath the castle, the one the fox had led me to and Idonia had warned me from. I should leave the matter alone, but my curiosity was too strong to let it rest entirely.

She drew away from me and bit her lip, then nodded. I smiled. So she was a little curious, at least. I was tempted to take the key from her and perform my own investigations this evening, but I knew that if she found out, she would not forgive me.

"Tell me, Liesl. I promise I will not go without you. Is it beneath the castle?"

"Yes," she said. "But how did you—?"

I cut her off. "It was an intuition." I was too embarrassed about the fox incident to tell her about it in full. "I was exploring one day and went down there. Idonia called me back right away. I got the feeling then that the room was forbidden."

She seemed satisfied with this answer and went back to listlessly picking at her food.

"Why did you not tell me about this key before?" I asked as we finished our dessert course later. Or, more accurately, I ate the delicious apple strudel Cook had made while Liesl picked hers apart, layer by flaky layer.

"I did not want you to have to bear this burden, little sister," she replied. "Though I confess, I feel a bit better now that you know."

A thought prickled at the back of my mind. It was a relief to know that this key had been bothering her, but Liesl had been poorly long before Bluebeard had given it to her. I said nothing of that sort, however. Instead, I smiled and assured her, "That's why I'm here, Liesl. And what sisters are for."

CHAPTER THIRTY-THREE

Anne's Diary

10 OCTOBER

The mystery of the key begins to haunt me as well. I have lain in bed half the night, unable to sleep with these thoughts. I've conjured many things that could be beyond that door . . . some splendid, some frightening. In the end, I believe I must know. I will tell Liesl that I have changed my mind and that we shall look inside the room. I am sure we shall laugh at ourselves, when we find that it is just a room full of more treasures, but I must know for sure what lies beyond the door unlocked by the golden key.

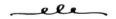

I was unable to convince Liesl to open the forbidden door, but I did get her to agree to our original plan, and I believe it was of some relief to both of us today. She still knows little of what happened between

Sebastian and me, and it was easier to hide my distress about it while doing something active. My struggle to think of him no more has not been victorious. Yet.

True to her word, Liesl set off with me after breakfast to explore the locked rooms of the castle. There was much to see. All along both the east and west wings are guest bedrooms and sitting rooms that we have not yet seen. All are well-furnished, though perhaps not quite as richly as the main parts of the castle. The library and the conservatory are still dearest to my heart, but these others are well worth exploring.

There were pieces of furniture of all shapes with intricate floral carvings made from rich, dark wood. Faded tapestries showing chivalrous scenes, oil paintings in ornate gilt frames, tarnished silver candlesticks, hand-knotted rugs in rich, jewel-like colors. Unfortunately, as much as I enjoyed seeing all these treasures, Liesl remained melancholy. She showed interest in only two items: an elaborately embroidered bedspread and a chess board that we decided to commandeer for our own use in the library.

As we entered the billiard room, which seemed not to have seen use for quite some time, I said, "We don't need to continue our explorations if you do not wish it."

"I wish it because you do," Liesl said. "I'm sorry, Anne. I'm not being a good companion to you. It is only that I'm very tired."

"If you're tired, we should rest. Let's return to the library. When you are feeling better, we can play a game of chess."

"I don't want to deprive you of this. I know how much you looked forward to seeing all these rooms. We can carry on."

I led her gently into the hall and locked the billiard room behind us. "Your husband will be gone for at least a week more. We have plenty of time to explore."

"If you don't mind, then," she said with reluctance. Her hand was quite cold when I took it and led her to the library, so I seated her in one of the upholstered chairs by the fireplace and covered her with a blanket. Then I began to set up the chess set on the small table between the two chairs.

"We shall have quite a merry winter here, don't you think?" I asked. "This library is the coziest place I can imagine, and we shall both become masters at chess."

She smiled wanly, closing her eyes. I worried for her again—could Idonia be making her ill somehow, even with me preparing her tea and the good cook making her food? I pushed the thought away, vowing to be more vigilant for whatever—and whoever—might be making her ill.

When I'd finished setting up the carved wooden chess pieces, I sat in the chair opposite hers. "Can I tell you a story?" I asked. "One of our favorite old tales?" I couldn't believe I hadn't thought of that before. The last time we'd spoken of fairy stories was the night of her proposal, when she recited Bearskin, but as girls, we used to take turns retelling our favorites every night. I began considering the possibilities—Rumpelstiltskin or Briar Rose or the White Snake. Surely one of them would cheer her.

She blanched and shuddered. "Anything but that. I shall hear no more of them." Before I could ask what she meant, she forced a smile and said, "How about a game? If we start now, we might well become chess masters by spring, as you said."

I agreed, and we did play a game, but neither of our hearts were in it. We abandoned it when each of us had lost so many pieces that we were not sure either of us could win.

It was then almost teatime, so I went down to the kitchens and made tea for us. Cook smiled as she slipped me a plate of fresh-baked scones. "How is the mistress?" she asked.

"She is a little tired," I said. "I do not think she has been sleeping well."

"I'm sorry to hear that. She is such a lamb, I can't imagine anything would be troubling her. Perhaps she misses the master."

"Is the master away like this often?" I asked, attempting to sound only vaguely curious. Cristina had heard from the other servants that this was unusual for him, but I hoped Cook might give me a different answer. Or even some clue as to where he had gone.

"I cannot really say, dear. I have not served him long."

"Really?" I asked. For Cook's warm smile and command of her kitchen seemed as much fixtures of the place as the great iron stove or the copper pots hung from the wall.

"Yes, I only began here a couple of years ago. He did not travel much at first—did not leave for more than two days at a time until a few months ago."

My heart sank a little. Cook was the friendliest servant, but for all her dismissing of the other servants' belief in curses and ghosts, she had not been here long enough to know. She could not tell me if Amalie had suffered the way Liesl suffered now.

When I returned to the library with the tea tray, Liesl had dozed off in front of the fire. I carefully removed the chess board and placed the tea on the table, but decided not to wake her, instead taking a scone and sitting on my chair in a way both Liesl and Idonia would call "unladylike."

I gazed into the fire and, despite my best efforts, found my mind wandering to Sebastian. I cannot get the feel of his hands on me as we danced—or that fire I saw in his eyes when I thought he might kiss me—out of my head. I've had some rather unladylike thoughts about him, too.

When Bluebeard came to our village, I thought myself wholly unready for marriage. I am still rather young—though I know girls my age who have already been married for a year—but I am not sure I feel so unready now. At least, I sometimes imagined it with Sebastian. I do not even know if that is proper or possible now. When I was a goatherd, a match to a gardener who worked an estate as great as Bluebeard's might have been a reach for me, but now that I am nearly as much of a lady as my sister—or at least expected to act and dress like one—am I supposed to look for a match with someone like Herr Franz or Herr Gustav?

That is what I thought I wanted when I first danced with them, but I cannot imagine a lifetime with either of them. With Sebastian, I . . . But he made it clear that shall never happen when we fought at the masquerade. He pushed me away, into the arms of any noble who would dance with me, all while giving vague admonitions of danger and hints at the dark past of this place. I was a fool to think he cared for me at all, and to let myself begin to care for him.

Liesl cried out in her sleep, interrupting my thoughts, and I got up and woke her. Her deep brown eyes went wide, frantically searching the room before they settled on me.

"It was a nightmare," she whispered, and I embraced her.

"All is well," I said as I tucked the blanket around her again. I pushed her teacup into her cold hands and seated myself again. "Is this why you have been so tired? Have you been having nightmares?"

She hesitated before saying, "I do not sleep well in my room. Yes, I suppose you could call them nightmares."

I wondered if this was something I dared not speak of—that she was in the room alone, now that Bluebeard was gone—and blushed. He had his own quarters, and, in truth, I knew nothing of their sleeping arrangements. Nor was I supposed to know anything about what went on between a husband and wife in their bed-chamber. How was I to know whether his leaving should make her sleep better or worse?

"What's wrong?" I had foolishly thought that she would be back to her old self after telling me her secret about the key, but she was just as weak and pale today. Perhaps even worse. "Can I help in any way? I think a good night's sleep will do wonders for you. Perhaps there are herbs in the garden to help—"

"No," she said sadly. "I have tried a few things, but nothing helps. But perhaps . . . "

"Yes?"

"Perhaps if you were to spend the night in my room, that might be a comfort to me."

I smiled. It would be like when we shared our bed in the loft—it seemed part of another lifetime, though it had not really been so long ago. "Of course, if you wish it." Maybe we could even tell each other stories again, though she was so against the idea earlier in the day.

Her face really brightened then—a bit of pink came back to her cheeks, and her lips formed almost a smile. "Thank you."

"Of course," I said. Had I known it would be so easy to make her happy again, I would have offered days ago.

CHAPTER THIRTY-FOUR

Anne's Diary

11 October

I see now why Liesl is so pale and tired. I did not sleep a wink last night, for we experienced many disturbances. Things that should have been impossible. She says they began her first night in the house but have grown much stronger since Bluebeard left. When she asked him about them, he had her half-convinced they were only nightmares.

First, the window kept coming open, letting harsh drafts of cold air enter the room no matter how many times I got up and latched it. Even when the window was shut, the candles flickered incessantly, leaving us in moments of darkness before bursting back to life. The door, too, would not stay closed. I even locked it once, only to find the deadbolt slid back and the door creaking open a few minutes later. When I closed it once more, heart thumping against my ribs, I thought I glimpsed the white-tipped tail of a fox in the hall. Clearly, the lack of sleep was weighing on me, too. Making me see things that were not there.

We also smelled things, heard things. Liesl and I huddled together in the bed, trembling in fear every time we smelled lavender or roses or dahlias, whenever we heard sweet notes of a piano or a woman's laughter.

"I thought I was going mad," Liesl whispered to me. "But you can hear and smell and see what has been happening to me every night, too."

"Liesl, why did you not tell me?"

"If I was mad, I didn't want anyone to know. Least of all you."

"You aren't mad, unless we have somehow both gone mad and are imagining the same horrid things. But even if you were, Liesl, I would help you. You must not keep secrets from me." I felt a prickle of guilt as I remembered how little I had told her these last weeks.

A cold draft washed over us again, this time without the window opening at all, and we both shuddered. "Do you believe in ghosts?" Liesl asked, her voice a whisper in my ear.

I hadn't the day before. Now, I didn't know. "Could the servants be doing this?" Could one of them somehow find humor in terrifying the mistress of the castle half to death?

"No," she said. "There have been several nights when I left my room, and no one was there. The castle is haunted—there can be no other explanation."

My thoughts flew again to Bluebeard's past wives. Amalie was said to have disappeared. But I knew nothing of Rosalind or Margaret or any others who might have come before. If something terrible had killed them here, might their spirits have become tied to the castle, unable to journey on to their eternal rest? Yet more secrets I'd kept from Liesl, but I did not want to scare her more by untangling them all now.

"If these are ghosts," I said, "who are they? And what do they want?"

"Why must a ghost desire anything beyond terrorizing the innocent?" Liesl asked. She held tight to the edge of the blanket and kept her eyes on her lap.

Thanks to Silvia sneaking them to me, I have read my share of ghost stories. They always want something. Usually, there is some great trauma that ties them to our world—lost love, revenge, something they missed the chance to do in life. Of course, those stories make fickle guides; until last night, I did not think there was any truth in them at all.

"If they seek only to terrorize," I reasoned, "why have they not haunted me, too?"

Strangely, now that we had started speaking of them, the ghosts had gone rather inactive. The room was still perfumed in floral scents, but there were no more creaking doors or windows, no cold drafts, and the candlelight had steadied.

"Perhaps they only haunt the guilty."

I frowned. "What do you have to feel guilty about?"

She only shook her head.

I tried another tack. "How long has this been happening?"

"Since the first night I slept here," Liesl said, her voice small. "It follows me, room to room, and it does not matter what time of day or night I try to sleep . . . But it has worsened since Bluebeard left. Or perhaps . . . " She sat up straighter in bed. "Perhaps it grew worse after he gave me the key."

"The *key*," I hissed. "Where is it now?"

Liesl's shaking hands fiddled with the neckline of her nightgown and pulled out the golden key on a long chain. "Here."

"You've been wearing it?"

"Yes," she said. "I grow even more anxious if I do not keep it close. If I am not allowed to use it, surely it must not fall into the hands of anyone else."

It did not seem right to keep something that had given her such torment so close, but I said nothing of it. "What if—?" I cleared my throat and steadied my voice. "What if they want us to use it? Perhaps they want us to see whatever is hidden in that room."

As if responding to my words, the door creaked open again, just wide enough for either of us to slip through. "You see?" I said, getting out of bed. All was quiet and still again, and even the rosy scent had vanished.

"We should not be listening to ghosts. Or demons—whatever they are that are doing this to me."

"You can't continue like this," I said, my voice a little sharper than I meant it to be. "I've watched you start to waste away since we came here. You cannot go on without sleep. And you want the hauntings to stop, don't you? To be unafraid again?"

She stared at the open door and nodded.

"Is there not some part of you that needs to know what is there? What your husband is hiding from you?"

"Yes," she whispered.

"Then it's settled. We'll go down there and see what they want us to see." I started to walk toward the door, but Liesl scrambled out of the blankets and across the bed to grab my wrist.

"No," she said. "It will have to be tomorrow night." She nodded to the window. The curtains were still blown back, and the horizon had turned crimson with the first light of dawn. We agreed to wait until tonight's darkest hour, when the rest of the servants—Idonia in particular—will be fast asleep, and we can sneak down undisturbed.

The day passed slowly. We spoke no more of our plans for the darkest hour of the night, though I believe they weighed heavily on both of us. We stayed in the library most of the day, playing indifferent games of chess and working on embroidery. My little handkerchief with a galloping horse grew so horrid and tangled that I had to pull it all apart and begin anew. Even after I restarted and thought it was coming along better, I showed it to Liesl, and her hesitant, "Is it some kind of . . . animal?" convinced me the matter was hopeless.

To think how much this once would have upset me, back when my only worries were over snags in my embroidery and my lopsided flower arrangements.

Neither of us had appetites at breakfast or lunch, but I went down at the usual time in the afternoon and made the tea.

I must say that I think I was wrong about Idonia. She has not complained of me making tea for Liesl since that first day, and she has grown more attentive and seems kinder since Bluebeard left. Surely, if she were planning something against one of us, now would be the opportune moment, while the master of the castle is gone. But she merely asked if we were feeling well since we had skipped two meals, and encouraged us not to miss dinner, as Cook was preparing another surprise in the hopes of cheering up Liesl.

The surprise turned out to be venison stew. It was hearty and good, reminding me of meals we used to have at home after Gerard's successful hunts. My appetite returned, despite my nerves about our evening venture, and I ate greedily. Eventually this endless day ended, and we retired to our rooms. I wanted to stay with Liesl, but she said I should go to my own chambers so that I could hope to get a little sleep before tonight. Of course, I am far too anxious to sleep.

We are to meet at the northwest tower at the witching hour, and we shall open the door beneath the castle and see whatever secrets the room holds. I shall laugh—in both relief and good humor—if it is only fine furnishings like the rest of the castle, or a special wine cellar, or some other mundane thing. But then I remember the ghosts . . .

I hoped that writing this out would help me pass the time, and indeed it has. I needed no help staying awake, but now time has moved so fast it is nearly the agreed-upon hour. I must take my dark cloak and candelabra and meet Liesl in the hall. Finally, this mystery shall be laid to rest, and we can both be at peace again.

CHAPTER THIRTY-FIVE

Bluebeard's Diary | Margaret

11 MAY, 13TH YEAR OF QUEEN THERESA I

Whispers followed me for years after Thekla. Some stemmed from her suitors, who were angry first that I had taken her from them, and then that I had allowed her to die while birthing my child, who was tragically stillborn. That was the tale I spun for them, anyway. It may not have been enough. Perhaps staging a funeral, as I did with Cacilie, would have helped, but I did not want others to share in her death. She is mine alone.

Others knew that I'd had three wives in two decades. They either thought me unlucky or callous, and I decided it was best to wait some years before seeking a new wife. Now, I'm sure almost none but I remember their names.

But of course, I became restless and lonely in due course, and knew it was time to start the hunt again. I did not want another Thekla—in any case, I did not think another like her would be born here in a generation or two. Always, I have longed for a companion, someone who can ascend the mortal realm with me and sit at my side. But now I see such is not my fate.

If I could not have a wife strong enough to join me, I would find one meek enough to obey.

I stopped searching other men's arms at balls and feasts, looking for the brightest stars among the debutantes. Instead, I began traveling the outskirts of ballrooms and sitting rooms, examining the wallflowers. It took a few months, but in time I found Margaret.

I watched her for weeks before I spoke to her. No matter the event—a grand ball, a concert, a quiet dinner at the home of a nobleman—she held a book in her hands. Her honey-brown eyes rapidly skimmed the words, and she always sat at the edge of her seat, as if the book gripped her and pulled her forward. Her hair was the color of straw, and her skin was freckled, but her round cheeks and Rubenesque form are what appealed to me.

She did not attend these events to find suitors, and it was clear she took no joy in them. Margaret only dressed in silks and adorned herself with jewels because she was ordered to by her red-faced, curmudgeonly father. A woman like that could be just what I needed. One who would be a companion to me, but who would do whatever I said. If only Thekla had not failed me, I would have a true partner with whom to share my gift. Instead, I am forced to find her opposite. A wife who will not ask questions about those who came before her, who would dare not defy me.

Margaret was obedient to her father, and she was so absorbed in her novels that surely she would care little for my past. She might not even pull her gaze from her books long enough to notice my bluish beard or my never-aging face.

When I first attempted to court her, she was not interested at all. I did not mind the challenge, as it has been so long since I had to work for anything. After many failed attempts—asking her to dance, sending her flowers, visiting her home with a lovely horse in tow and asking her to ride the countryside with me—I realized the key to her heart was those books she was always buried in.

I began writing poems. Well, I did not write them, but I sponsored a struggling writer a few towns over. In return for the capital to begin publishing his silly love stories, I had him write a series of twelve poems about Margaret that I could pass off as my own creations.

It worked beautifully. After she'd read only half the poems, she was mine.

I gave her the others during our first six months of marriage, and after that, I began buying her books. She was a good wife, dressing in fine garments the way she should, planning the splendid events hosted at the castle despite them giving her no joy. After I declined to answer the first few times, she never asked me about my past again. Every spare moment was spent curled up near the fireplace in the library, reading books.

With things between us going so well, I hesitated to ruin it all with my test of her obedience. After all, I had misjudged others before her. I had meant to test her in the first few months of marriage, but I kept putting it off. Until, after I had run out of poems, she began spending more and more of her time within the worlds of her books. I tried to track down the poet again, but his silly book had done well somehow, and he'd moved to one of Westenfall's neighboring kingdoms. Margaret would surely be able to tell if anyone else wrote her poems. She began to sigh, sometimes, and ask where the romantic man who had first courted her had gone. No doubt all those books had given her such ideas.

I decided then that I must test her. If she passed, well and good. If not, I would be done with her, and with the matter of the poems and the wistful sighs.

Telling her I was going away for a few weeks, I gave her the keys to my castle, including the small golden key that unlocked the room where I carried out the rituals. Where I won for myself that which the alchemist who used to live in that room could not. I told Margaret she had free reign over the castle, but she must not use that key. She shrugged and bid me adieu before turning her nose back into a book.

I stayed near, in the next village, so that if anything should go wrong, I might find out and take care of any problems. It would be easy enough to claim her mad if she raved to anyone about the room. No such rumors reached me. Relieved, I rode back to my castle after only one week, as usual.

One of the servants rushed to me when I entered my home, babbling that my wife had taken ill and that they did not know where to send for me. Calmly, I let myself be led to her room, then dismissed all the servants. Margaret laid in her bed, weak and pale, but she was awake.

"What have you done?" she asked.

I said nothing, only held her gaze. Her honey eyes, wide with horror, searched mine.

"Why?" The word was small, pleading.

I had told no one for years, so I did not mind telling her then. She did not faint or flinch away as I revealed the details of the ritual, the price I had paid for all I have gained.

When I finished, she said only, "I am to be next?"

"You could not obey me," I answered, and she did not understand. If she had understood, perhaps I could trust her to tell no one. But I could see that I was a monster to her. A monster who she'd thought wrote her poems of his love.

She sat up in bed. "I thought as much," she said. "You never loved me, did you? You just needed another life."

"In my way, perhaps I did care for you."

"Who wrote the poems?"

I saw no reason to lie to someone whose life was nearly at an end. Well, it was ending for her. It would soon be mine, her years only beginning for me. "A peasant who wanted to be a poet."

She nodded. When I took her hand and pulled her from bed, she did not fight me. Gently, I led her down the twisting staircase, to the room where I became more God than man. She did not sob or cry out, did not even turn her eyes away from the others. She said nothing until right before I took her life.

Margaret's light brown eyes bored into mine, and she said, "They are not gone, as you think. You have not defeated them. And you will not escape us, until justice has been done to you."

I am not easily frightened, after all I have seen, all I have done. But I must admit, a chill ran through me at her words. It was as if the eyes of the others stared into me, too. But I collected myself, and it was all over quick enough. Each time grows easier than the last.

CHAPTER THIRTY-SIX

Anne's Diary

12 OCTOBER

I cannot stop trembling. I've just seen the most horrible of sights. I do not know if I can believe them, and I am sure that I could not speak aloud of the horrors I have just experienced. I cannot escape them; even when I close my eyes, I see . . .

Perhaps if I write it, I can make some sense of what just happened and calm myself, though you must see the shaking of my hand in the strokes of my pen. To think that I believed our excursion would bring us peace. Now I think I shall never know peace again.

Liesl and I met at the door to the staircase that spirals down the northwest tower in the deadest hour of the night. We did not wish the servants to see what we were about, lest any of them should have been warned by Bluebeard to watch for us. And perhaps I had read too many books and liked the romanticism of discovering a hidden room after midnight. How foolish I was.

Though we had both been somber and lifeless all day, when we met and began down the staircase, we smiled, a little giddy at the thought of doing that which the owner of this castle forbade. I'd pushed the ghosts far out of my mind and half-convinced myself they had never been. My head was filled with visions of treasure—piles of coins from around the world, wooden chests that held bejeweled tiaras, gold chalices, silver platters, strings of pearls, and sparkling gemstones the size of eggs. I believe I read too many novels for my own good.

At the base of the staircase, when we stepped into the hall where no moonlight could reach, we both sobered. I gently took her wrist and led her to the door where the fox had once led me. I no longer thought that I was mad or had imagined the fox; surely it was another trick by whatever haunted Liesl's rooms at night. Whatever wanted us to do this.

"Do you have the key?" I whispered to Liesl in the dark hallway. I held out my candlestick, and the orb of its flames glinted off the gold surface of the key in her outstretched palm.

"Yes," she said. I watched her hand feel along the rough wooden door for the keyhole. Her fingers stopped in the middle of the door. "There's something engraved here," she whispered.

I held the candelabra up higher to illuminate the engraving. It read:

A bright eye indicates curiosity;
A black eye, too much

Liesl's pale face turned to me, flickering in the golden candlelight. "We should not do this."

Similar doubts plagued me. Surely it was not wise to do that which a husband forbade, even more foolish to do what wretched ghosts asked. "If you fear what he might do if he finds out—if you do not think we can hide what we've done—then let us forget the idea."

"I do not think he would hurt me, or at least he has not done so before. But—I do not know why—I am afraid. I feel chilled to the core, Anne."

She wrapped her icy hand around mine, and I began to retreat down the corridor, a little relieved, for I was full of trepidation now too. "As you wish. We will go on as if we never came here."

Halfway down the hall, Liesl yanked her hand from mine, and I heard her footsteps retreat from me, back toward the door.

"Liesl," I hissed. "Where are you going?" I lifted my skirts and ran after her, trying to keep my steps light to avoid waking anyone, though I doubted the sound could travel through the thick stone walls.

"If this will make them stop, I must do it," I heard Liesl say, and then there was a click. "I've unlocked it," she said breathlessly as I caught up to her with the light. "Oh, to sleep again."

"Do not frighten me like that," I said, trying to catch my breath.

"Are you ready?" she asked. There was a glint of something in her eyes as she turned to me. At the time, I thought it was curiosity, as the engraving on the door described. Now I see that it must have been an ounce of madness—madness had driven her back to the door, to the room of secrets. Warner told me once that people can go mad if they do not sleep, and perhaps, had Liesl been well-rested, or had I not been so dangerously curious, we would not have dared to enter that room. If only we could turn back time.

I could hear my heart beating quite loud and fast as she waited for my answer. Finally, I nodded. "I am ready." She swung open the door.

The room was pitch-dark, and at first, we could see nothing. Liesl and I stepped inside slowly.

"The floor is wet," she said, and I heard her skirts rustle as she lifted them above her ankles.

I nodded to myself. It was not surprising that rainwater had entered here. We were below ground, after all. Carefully, I lifted my skirts with the hand that was not holding the candle.

Without meaning to, I'd lowered the candelabra closer to the floor, to the puddle in which we stood, while wrestling with my skirts.

"It's . . . red," Liesl said, her voice beginning to shake. "Deep red, like wine."

I took two small steps further into the room, holding the candle as far out as I could. "Red like blood!" I gasped. Our eyes strained to see further, then Liesl cried out, and I recoiled.

For there, further into the room, we found what had become of Bluebeard's previous wives.

Six figures hung along the walls, their blood pooled together at their feet. I felt I would be sick, or perhaps faint, but some dark place inside me would not let me leave the room until I had seen their faces. Liesl clung to me, and I felt her whole body shake in fear as we stepped further into the room, but she did not turn back.

I gasped and had to swallow, trying to steady my stomach, when I saw that they were hung, not by rope around their necks as I had first thought, but by great iron hooks through their shoulders. Empty hooks lined the other wall, waiting for more wives. For Liesl and me. I shuddered. The smell was horrid, indescribable, and the blood was sticky beneath our feet. Their dresses were stained dark with blood that somehow never clotted. The worst part of all was the horror on each of their faces. Never have I seen such ghastly expressions.

Now I think I shall never stop seeing them. Their terror and pain have been seared on my soul.

The cool, stale air and perhaps some bit of dark magic had preserved their faces. I could not guess how long they had hung in that room, but each could have been placed there but a few days ago, if not for the pallor of their faces, the horrible way their mouths were contorted in fear, and their blood, drained and all mingled together in a great pool on the floor. They were all beautiful, all elegantly dressed, all young. A horrid, twisted mirror of ourselves. The six of them, dead, and the two of us, alive but waiting to join them.

In the center of the room stood a stone table—an altar, I realized—holding a few scrolls of parchment, burned stubs of candles, and a large knife that made me quite ill to behold.

"I—I'm going to be sick," Liesl said, just as I felt the same. "We need to leave."

We turned, the candlestick ahead of us and Liesl's fingers still digging into my arm. I was rather afraid to turn from them—for surely their spirits are what have plagued Liesl every night—but I needed to be anywhere but that room. Our feet splashed horridly in the blood as we hurried out, and then there was a different splash, of something falling.

"The key!" Liesl exclaimed. "We must find it or—or he'll know!" Her eyes widened in the glow of the candle flame.

"Yes, we must." I moved the candelabra back and forth near her feet. I spotted it, and she hesitated for a moment, then reached into the sticky blood with two fingers and pulled out the golden key.

We left the room quickly, slamming the door shut behind us. Liesl locked it with shaking hands, and we both collapsed in a pile of blood-stained skirts and sat against the door.

"Is it real?" Liesl asked, breathless. "What we saw?"

"Yes," I said, barely forcing the sound through my parched throat. "It was."

"What do we do?" She turned to me, her eyes wide. I remembered my promise; I must do whatever I can to keep us safe—and happy, though that seems impossible now.

"We can never tell a soul," I said, realizing that was the first step. "The servants . . . they must already suspect something is amiss. Cook says they are only superstitious, but they have done naught to warn you, so we mustn't trust them." That wasn't entirely true, of course. Sebastian had tried to warn me, but I shivered with fear to think he might know of the horrors of that room and yet still stay in this murderous man's employ.

Liesl nodded solemnly. I hoped my plan could save us.

"We must wash the blood from our clothes, if we can, or perhaps just destroy them. In any case, I never wish to wear this again," I said, shuddering. I could feel that I might break down at any moment and grasping for a plan—some way to hide what we now knew—was the only way I knew to calm myself. And hopefully, Liesl as well.

"And our hands, and the key," Liesl said, unfurling her palm, which was stained red and still held the key, which was now slick with blood, too. I hoped she would no longer wear it about her neck, now that she knew what it protected.

"Yes," I said. "We must pretend as if everything is the same. I will write to Klaus and ask Father and our brothers to visit, and to take us far away from here before Bluebeard returns. Until then, we must,"—I clasped her wrists—"we *must* do whatever it takes so that the servants do not know we entered the room. We cannot know whom among them is his ally in this wickedness."

Liesl nodded. "I think I might be sick," she said, and then she was, and I was, too.

When the violence of our stomachs had subsided, I noted, "We shall also need to clean up this hallway."

After we'd finished, we quietly went upstairs and slipped into our quarters. I hid my dress in a trunk, planning to remove the blood with cool water tomorrow, and washed my hands and feet with the water from my toilette. My body has not ceased trembling since we left that room, but my mind has calmed now that I've written what happened. As long as we can make Bluebeard believe that we never ventured to that room, we shall be safe. Father and Klaus and the rest will come and take us far from these haunted halls.

There was a knock on my door, and I knew it was Liesl, who had been as unable to sleep as I. Fears and visions of those poor women's faces haunted my every waking minute; how much worse would my dreams be?

I opened the door to her panicked face. "The key," she said. "The golden key—it is stained with blood I cannot remove."

"Come in," I said. Dawn approached, and I worried the servants might overhear.

She handed me the key. It was dry, smooth, and warmed by her hand, the way gold should be, but much of it was stained scarlet with blood. We scrubbed it in the remaining water from my toilette, used soap, tried every kind of fabric, but to no avail. The stain did not lessen or lighten in the slightest.

"It's no use!" Liesl cried. "The key—it must be enchanted, or cursed, as that room was. When he returns, he'll kill me, and I shall end up in that room, with—with—" She burst into tears, and I held her, stroking her hair, her back.

"Shh, shh, Liesl," I said. "Be still. I shall write to Klaus and send the letter with the first post. There is still time before Blu—before *he* returns. Time for Father and our brothers to make the journey here and rescue us."

I thought of the ghosts, too. They had wanted us to discover what happened to them. Did they want more from us? Or were they merely trying to save us, having had no one to warn them before Bluebeard enacted his bloodlust upon them?

"Do you believe that?" Liesl said, her face brightening a little. "Truly?"

"Yes," I said. "I do."

"You should go, Anne," Liesl said. "Leave here while you can—"

"I could never leave you after all this. If our family does not arrive in time, we shall find a way to leave—together. We can come up with some excuse to leave the castle and not return."

I said it with more confidence than I felt. I hadn't left the estate since first setting foot on it, and didn't even know what the nearest town was, much less the way home. And surely Bluebeard, with all his influence and resources, could easily find us wherever we fled. No, our best course was to call on our family to help us.

The same difficulties with our escape must have been going through her mind because she didn't look at all convinced. "Maybe if we take a couple of horses—"

She shook her head. "He lent his horses to a friend for a hunting party while he was away. The stables are empty."

My heart sank. With horses, we might have had a chance to put enough distance between us and him. But I hid my despair the best I could and promised, "We *will* find a way out of this, Liesl. I think you should stay here in my room for the rest of the night, and we shall take comfort in each other's presence to help us sleep."

She nodded and crawled into my bed. She fell asleep after some time, but I did not. Instead, I've written this account, and my letter to Klaus. It should arrive in time for our family to come to us before

Bluebeard returns from his trip, but the fear that it will not has kept me sleepless the whole night through.

CHAPTER THIRTY-SEVEN

Letter from Liesl

12 OCTOBER

Oh Mother, what have I done?

I thought I'd found my Bearskin, but instead, I wed a different character from that wretched story: the devil himself.

Anne and I have just learned the grisly truth about my husband: he had six wives before me, and killed them all, spilling their blood in a sickening room beneath the castle. To what purpose, I do not know. Neither do I know why he has not killed me yet, or why he should give me the key to his slaughter room. I cannot even feel relieved that I remain of sound mind, and my sleepless nights did not indicate madness, because I feel far more ill than I did before. How could we all have been feasting and dancing and laughing each night when below us lay such horror, when it was all built on a foundation of blood and death?

I only know that we must escape before he returns. Anne is writing to our family, but will it be enough? If not, we can try to flee, but how will we manage it? My husband is a fierce hunter with near-unlimited wealth and connections. He will find us, wherever we go.

Oh, I am wretched. I have endangered them all with my stubborn, selfish pursuit of a better life. Mother, I must ask that if you have any powers to help us from the afterlife, use them now. For all of us to come through this alive and unharmed, we will need nothing short of a miracle.

Please, Mother. Help us if you can.

Liesl

CHAPTER THIRTY-EIGHT

Letters from Anne

12 & 13 OCTOBER

D earest Klaus,

You must come to us at once and take us from here. Gather Father and our brothers together and make haste to visit us. I do not know if I have the time or strength to write the details, but Liesl and I have discovered the most horrid of things about the master of this castle.

You remember, dear brother, that you told me of the whisperings you had heard of Bluebeard's past wives? Suffice it to say that we have discovered what became of them, and to avoid the same fate ourselves, you must come to our aid. We shall not live to see you again if you do not. Please, Klaus. Make haste.

Your loving sister,

Anne

Klaus—

You must come to us immediately. I hope this reaches you promptly after my last letter, if not before. I will send it via the fastest rider I can find. It is a matter of life or death.

We received word that Bluebeard is coming home early. If you leave at once, you may make it in time to rescue us, for we hope to hold out with him a day or two. If you do not . . . we will escape on our own, and you may have to find us in the woods surrounding the estate or the closest village—before Bluebeard does. We have little confidence in our success.

Please. Come at once.

Anne

CHAPTER THIRTY-NINE

Anne's Diary

14 OCTOBER

I have been too distressed to write these last couple of days, but now I feel I must. I fear horrible things may be on the horizon for us, and though I do not know for whom I write, perhaps this will help someone. Someday.

Bluebeard returned in the wee hours of the morning. I watched out my window as he rode up and the servants tended to his horse, for I could not sleep. The image of those dead faces and of the empty hooks would not leave me. Upon seeing Bluebeard return, I scurried into Liesl's room to tell her.

She opened the door and ushered me inside. She had not slept either, though the ghosts had been mercifully quiet the past few days.

"He is here," I hissed.

"I know," Liesl said vacantly.

"Why did he return early?" Yesterday I had Liesl convinced we should run this evening, but now that he had returned... "What are we to do? Should we run into the woods?"

She looked at me with her hollow eyes and said, "There is nothing we can do, but pray he does not ask for the key."

"You must see that we need to escape. We must leave here. Father and our brothers won't make it for days. It is up to us."

Liesl shook her head slowly. "We don't know this land. How would we make our way in it? He would find us, and we have no one to protect us," she said. "We must stay and pray for the best."

I felt as if fear had stolen my sister from me. She stood before me, but the spark of life inside her had been snuffed out. I wanted to slap her, to see if I could jolt her into herself once again. But I could see as well as she that now that Bluebeard had arrived, the door to our escape had closed.

"I shall return to my room," I said.

She patted my hand. "Things will turn out well, Anne. We must believe they shall."

She spoke strong words, but a tear slipped down her cheek. I embraced her and then hurried back to my room, where I waited impatiently to break my fast.

He was not at breakfast, as he had business to attend to, which was some small relief. But we are told he will join us for dinner an hour from now.

Today was another long one that has passed slowly and in great fear. I spent much of it walking through the forest. The way the trees encroach upon the castle and its grounds never seemed so ominous to me before. They have trapped us, isolated us. I do not know what there is beyond the woods or even in what direction the nearest village lies. How am I to run for help without becoming hopelessly lost?

And I am afraid it will be needed. I have heard nothing from Klaus and worry my first letter may have gone astray. If the second reached him, I've calculated that the earliest they can arrive, if they set off promptly, is three days from now. Are we to spend three whole days in the company of Bluebeard, pretending we know nothing and hoping he does not ask for the key?

Before I entered the woods, I packed a bit of food from the kitchens, along with my two plain gardening dresses, into a satchel. Then I concealed the satchel in the garden on the hill. Only Sebastian and I know it has been restored, so I do not think anyone will look there, and doing *something* to prepare for the inevitable worst calmed me a little.

The forest is lovely now, and I think I would have quite enjoyed my long walk today, had it been under less dire circumstances. The trees were radiant in crimson and flame-orange and gold. Fallen leaves and acorns crunched beneath my feet as I walked. Those birds that had not yet flown south sang in the trees, and the squirrels buried nuts for the coming winter. Even its smell, of wet earth and slight decay, was a comfort.

I hoped that if I walked farther along one of the deer paths through the woods than I had ever gone before, I would catch sight of a village or cottage or even a cave—somewhere we could run to.

But I walked until noon before turning around and saw no such haven. Even if I had, I am not sure it would have helped. Bluebeard is a great hunter. I have no doubt he would steal the breath from our lungs if he knew what we know about him.

After my walk, I went to the kitchens to help Cook. She was making a rich dessert from chocolate and cherries in celebration of Bluebeard's return. I'm sure it will be sumptuous, and I'm equally sure I shall be unable to swallow a bite. In fact, pulling pits from the flesh of the cherries and the way their juice stained my fingers made me feel quite ill. I also couldn't help thinking about Cook—I don't want to suspect her, but could she know what he really is? Anyway, I had to excuse myself after pitting only a few cherries.

She was so warm and welcoming to us, and how could she have been if she knew what fate might await us? Her heart must be as black and twisted as Bluebeard's if she cared for us so and then allowed us to be harmed without a breath of the truth she knew. And if she is to be believed—and I do want to believe her, as much as I distrust everyone now—she has not been here long.

Idonia has been with the castle the longest. She must know something, even if it is only that the wives disappeared. I thought again of her poison garden, but the raw terror on the women's faces surely could not have been from taking poison. That sort of death would have been merciful. Still, how had I ever grown to trust her after she concealed that horrible room from me, after I discovered her garden of death?

Cristina, I am sure, knows nothing. She has not been at the castle long and is one of the cheeriest of the servants. Liesl's lady's maid also came to the castle when we arrived. I hope they will be safe, whatever happens to us. As for the other servants . . . I don't know. They certainly whisper and have their superstitions, but would none of them find it in their hearts to tell us if they had known?

Of course, Sebastian did warn me. If only I had listened. I was so angry with him after seeing what lies beneath the castle, thinking he might have tried harder to warn us if he knew the truth. But perhaps imminent death has put me in a more forgiving mood. It is possible he did not know the full truth—he said as much, after all. And even if he did and had told me, would I have believed him? Or would I have been tempted to look for myself, to see with my own eyes, and ended up right where we are now?

But he also said it was too late for Liesl, that I should take whatever way out I could, and for that I cannot forgive him. Did he not see how I love her, how betraying her would rend my heart in two? There was a moment in the woods today, even, when I thought that I might take the rations from the garden on the hill and go off into the woods on my own. I could leave this place and its terrors behind me, assume a new identity, and start a new life. Bluebeard might never learn that I knew of his secret. My traitorous mind considered it for minutes that stretched long, but my heart would not let me. I cannot abandon Liesl. She and Klaus are the dearest people in the world to me.

Before coming back to my quarters, I did remember something.

In one of the rooms we explored, there were three little jeweled daggers in a case. They looked ornamental and were not much bigger than my quill here, but when I tested one on the pad of my thumb,

I'd found it quite sharp. This morning, I asked Liesl for the ring of keys and took the daggers from the room. I sewed them into the sleeves of my dress, and I admit that the weight of them against my arms gives me some small comfort, though I do not think myself capable of using them, even against a wolf like Bluebeard.

I have done all I can now, as little as that is. It grows late, so I must tuck this into my sash before the ink is quite dry and go down to dine with my sister and her devil of a husband.

CHAPTER FORTY

Anne's Diary

14 OR 15 OCTOBER

I do not know how anyone shall read this, as the parchment is so drenched that much of the ink slides across the page as I write, and it is so dark that I can scant see the quill meet the page. I also do not know how Liesl can slumber now, with the rain pounding the ground all around us, nor whether we shall still be here, hidden in this thicket of trees, when the sun rises. Bluebeard might find us first.

I feel as if I know nothing at all.

Perhaps I shall write what I do know—how we came to be here; how Liesl and I were able to survive thus far, to steal a few more hours of life from Bluebeard's grasp.

It started at dinner. Bluebeard was quieter than usual, and neither of us were able to make much conversation, so it passed slowly and in silence. Peals of thunder filled in our silence. The rain beat against the windows, obscuring the view and making me feel even more closed-in and desolate.

After finishing his last bites of dessert, Bluebeard wiped his mouth on his napkin and stood. Then, as if he'd just thought of it, he turned and asked Liesl for the keys.

She patted the pocket of her dress and then feigned confusion. "I have left them in my room."

"Bring them to the library, then," Bluebeard said gruffly and stalked off to the staircase.

Liesl had no choice but to obey. I went with her to retrieve them, and she slipped the golden key onto the ring, turning it to bury the key in the middle of all the others. It was a rather small key, and we hoped he would not notice the dull reddish stain across its golden surface.

We were not to have such luck, however. Upon returning them to him, Bluebeard slowly examined each key, as if ensuring they were in the same order as when he left us. As each one fell against the others with a clink, his eyes flicked to Liesl. She looked calm, working on her embroidery, though I'm sure her hands trembled and her heart thundered just as mine did.

He stopped on the golden key, and I tried to look as innocent as I could while holding my breath.

Slowly, he turned on his heel and held up the key. "I am disappointed, wife," he said to Liesl, and I was so afraid I thought I might faint. His eyes were hard and cold, though his voice was calm. "I truly believed you better than the others."

He crossed the room to her, and I jumped out of my chair. "It was my fault! I—I was helping Cook, and the key became s-stained with cherry juice."

A harsh, booming laugh escaped Bluebeard. "These lies!"

Standing and stepping in front of me, Liesl said, "You must not listen to her, my liege. I acted alone."

Bluebeard ripped the sapphire ring from Liesl's finger. "It matters not. You'll both pay," he said, then drew the sword at his waist with a flash of steel and a metallic ring.

"Please, we will tell no one what we saw," Liesl pleaded. She reached a tentative hand out to him. "I—I love you."

He struck her cheek with the hand holding the sword. She collapsed to the floor and began to weep. "Lies," he said. "I will have no more of them." He raised the sword, pointing it at her heart, and Liesl tried to back away, one hand pressed to her rapidly bruising cheek. "To the dungeon with you, traitor wife."

"Wait!" I called out, mind racing to think of something, anything I could say to stay his hand.

"Worry not. It shall be your turn next," he growled.

"It is only that—that you must let us say our final prayers!"

Bluebeard lowered the sword an inch. "Why should I?" he spat.

"You must slay us—I see that—but must you damn our souls as well? And in so doing, perhaps also your own?" I was grasping, but the words must have struck a chord with him, for he sheathed the sword.

"Ten minutes I'll give you," he said. "That and no more, so make peace with your maker quickly. You shall not leave this room."

He stalked out, slamming the door behind him, then locked us in.

I helped Liesl stand and examined the mark on her face. It was an angry red, with faint purple bruising already spreading beneath. "Are you alright?"

"Does it matter?" she asked. "That was very brave, Anne, but what was the point? You just delayed the inevitable."

"No," I said. "We're going to escape." I strode to the window with more confidence than I felt. We would need to smash one of the stained-glass windows and jump to the ground.

"We're two stories up!" Liesl said. "We'll never survive."

"We'll have a better chance than we do here," I said. "Now go listen at the door and see if he's still there. If he isn't, barricade it with something."

She obeyed, and I began to search the room for something heavy enough to throw through the window, anything that could break through the solder holding the glass pieces together. I chose a heavy brass candelabra and grabbed it in two hands.

"Bluebeard? My love?" Liesl asked through the door.

There was no response, so she nodded to me and pushed a chaise lounge against the door. I threw the candlestick at the window as hard as I could. I winced at the sound of shattering glass—it had broken out a few pieces but did not make a gap wide enough for either of us to jump through. Rain fell in sheets outside the window, and the room grew cold and damp.

"Quick, find something else!" I said as I heaved a giant tome at the window.

Liesl grabbed a small marble bust from a shelf and used it to smash out the remaining pieces until there was a wide enough hole. But then, after looking down, she backed away slowly. "I cannot do this, Anne."

Footsteps echoed out in the hall. "We have no choice. Remember our riding lessons? Roll to soften the impact. You can do it!" Then I half-shoved her through the window.

She rolled clumsily on the wet grass, and I made sure she was able to stand before stepping onto the windowsill myself and crouching in the gap we had made. It was a long drop, but it was also our only way out. I took one last look at the view. Despite the rain, a few fireflies winked in the dark safety of the forest. I took a deep breath of rain-heavy air and jumped right as I heard the key in the library door again.

I landed on my feet, knees bent, and did a half-roll. I felt the elbow of my dress tear out and belatedly remembered the daggers I'd sewn into my sleeves. I'd turned my ankle, too, but there was no time to tend to that now. Liesl hauled me to my feet—she seemed unscathed by the fall—and we ran. Flashes of lightning and Bluebeard's angry cries followed us into the night.

We had just reached the base of the stone path up to the garden on the hill when we heard the dogs. "Hurry!" I pushed Liesl along and made a mad dash for the satchel of supplies I'd hidden earlier. Then we ran down the other side of the hill, slipping and sliding in the mud on our way down. The dogs' barking grew nearer, and I struggled to run on my injured ankle.

"They're gaining on us," Liesl said breathlessly.

"We have to lose them." I knew from my many wanderings through the woods that a river ran nearby, so I led us there, doing my best to weave through the trees and undergrowth in near-total darkness. Then I tied the satchel higher on my back and waded in, gasping as the cold water soaked my dress and chilled my legs.

"No, Anne, we'll catch our deaths of cold!"

"Better than to die by Bluebeard's hand," I said, then braced one knee on the riverbank and pulled her in beside me. I was shivering hard now, my teeth clicking together, but after Liesl recovered from the initial shock of cold, we waded along the river.

The current pulled at our skirts, slowing us, and I feared that it had been a mistake to enter the river. But the dogs—and undoubtedly by now, Bluebeard on his horse—kept gaining. It was a relief to follow a bend in the river, so the trees hid us from sight, just as the water concealed our scent from their keen noses.

"H-how much longer?" Liesl asked, her arms wrapped tight around her midsection. The rain continued to pelt us, so our sleeves and bodices were nearly as soaked as our skirts. A sliver of moon poked through the gray clouds, throwing the dark shadows beneath her eyes into starker relief.

I'd forgotten how ill she'd been these last weeks, that she did not have the strength she did when we were at home. Death awaited us at the castle, but we were not much better out here.

"We can get out now," I said, gently leading her to the opposite shore. "Our trail will have ended at the river. Hopefully, we've gone far enough to throw off the dogs."

Leaving the river with our heavy skirts was a struggle, but we made it and sat on the shore for a moment to catch our breaths.

"Perhaps we," I began, but was interrupted by a full-body shiver. "Perhaps if we come across an estate, one with horses, we could take one . . . "

Liesl shook her head. "Even if we came across such a poorly guarded estate, it's risky. And even if it were not, I do not want to become horse thieves in addition to . . . whatever else we are now."

I knew what she meant. Somehow, though we were running from a man who had killed six wives and strung them up beneath his castle, it felt as if *we* had done something wrong. I supposed it was a consequence of being on the run. It was worse for Liesl—I still shudder to think he was her husband, that she had sworn to love him. Oh, if only he had never seen us in the meadow!

We got to our feet and continued, far past exhaustion. We had to keep moving, both to put distance between ourselves and Bluebeard, and to keep the chill out of our bones. I kept us moving straight ahead as best I could, hoping we would come across a cabin or some sign of a nearby village, but there were only trees and shadows and the unrelenting rain.

"I cannot go on," Liesl said eventually, collapsing beneath a spruce tree. I was tired myself; each step took a Herculean effort.

"Alright, let's rest. We should eat something, too." I knelt beside her and opened the satchel. There was less in it than I remembered—and if I had thought ahead, I would have packed blankets or something with which to dry ourselves. Instead, there was only food, a wineskin, my gardening dresses, and a few candles that we didn't dare light right now.

The dresses, at least, were still dry. The last time I wore them was the day Sebastian and I finished the garden. What I would give to go back to that day! My problems then were paltry little things; I hadn't known then what danger we were in.

We peeled off our wet dresses and slipped the dry ones on. It did help some against the cold. Liesl looked a little silly, as hers was too wide in the hips and too tight in other places, but at least we were dry, and if anyone came across us, our dresses would not give us away as escaped noblewomen.

Liesl ate a small bread roll without much enthusiasm while I worked one of the daggers out of the sleeve of my ruined dress. Her eyes widened when she caught the flash of the cut ruby in its pommel. "Where did you get that?"

"From the room with the brown and gold curtains." I used the weapon to hack off boughs from a nearby pine tree, no doubt ruining the blade. Then I brought them to Liesl and said, "Here, cover yourself in these."

"I wish we c-could light a fire."

"Me too," I said. Even had there been no rain, there was too much danger of being seen to light one. "But sleep if you can. We'll want to be moving on soon."

She only nodded, her eyes already closed. After how long she went without, it is one small blessing that she can sleep now. I sat close beside her after cutting my own pine branches and endeavored to sleep. But every noise, every trickle of rain that made its way through the spruce tree and onto my head or arms, made me jump.

To think that in my wretched fairy stories, the woods are always dark and deep and full of danger. But now they're our only hope of refuge from a creature far worse than any wolf or bear.

I cannot help but think of Amalie now, running from the castle on a stormy night like this one. Now I see it was probably after she found what we did beneath the castle. She could have sat under a tree just like this, shivering and alone. I have that, at least. I am not alone. I wonder if she managed to escape him. Is she somewhere far from here, alive and well? Did she drown in the river or freeze in the forest? Or is she there, hung beneath the castle, one of the six faces that now haunts my every hour?

Unable to sleep with a mind so full of morbid thoughts, I pulled out this book. It has survived well despite the rain, and I thought writing of our misfortunes would calm me. It has, I think, for my eyes have grown heavy and, now that the rain has lightened, I shall try to slumber. Only for a short time, though—we must push on soon, lest Bluebeard catch up to us. Our last hope now is to evade his capture until our brothers come to save us.

CHAPTER FORTY-ONE

Letter from Bluebeard

15 OCTOBER

Dearest friends,

I write to inform you that my new bride and her sister are missing. I am afraid the girls are quite ill, and there was a misunderstanding between us which frightened the younger sister. They left the castle late last night, and I have been searching for them since. No doubt they have become lost in the woods.

If you should come across them, please contact me at once so I may take them safely home. Their illness has quite stirred their minds and given them nightmares, so be not alarmed if they rave about strange things. I believe with rest at home, they will recover to full health soon, but the longer they are lost, the greater risk their illness shall have on them. Whoever returns them safely to me shall, of course, have a rich reward from my personal treasury.

I worry for the girls, but it is a comfort to know I have so many friends who will help, however they can, to return them to me.

You have my deepest thanks,

Lord Wolfgang Conomor Marlais de Streifen

Bluebeard

CHAPTER FORTY-TWO

Anne's Diary

15 OCTOBER

We came upon a village this morning, and I was delighted to learn that we were not far from Franz's estate. I had not considered my ballroom partners before, but of course, they must help us. Seeking shelter with him was certainly a better plan than wandering the woods for days, even if coming to him in my desperation might sever any affection he may have once held for me.

A woman washing clothes in the river spotted us, and though she eyed our mud-stained dresses and bloodshot eyes with suspicion, she said nothing except to answer our questions and help orient us as to where we were. Not that it helped much, so little did we know of geography beyond our own village and Bluebeard's castle.

After thanking her, we left, following her instructions to skirt around the village without being seen. The weather had turned sunny again, though it is too far into autumn to be warm, and, unable to fully dry last night before changing, our dresses were still unpleasantly damp.

As we came within sight of the front gate to Franz's estate, Liesl asked, "Are you sure he will help us?"

"How can he not?" I asked, eyeing the garish green-and-purple bruise on her cheek. Even if he did not like me as much as I suspected he did, how could someone so gallant turn away two girls as gravely in distress as we were? It would go against all the chivalrous codes the nobility so loved.

The first challenge came when we reached the front gate. We waited a few minutes for a guard to pass by, and when he did, he took us for beggars and would not speak to us. Finally, after I detailed several conversations Franz and I had had while dancing, he became convinced that I might know his master. He sighed in frustration and returned to the estate to retrieve Franz.

Liesl seemed even worse after our night of running and sleeping in the rain. Her face was flushed with fever. She held the bars of the gate to support herself, her neck bent in exhaustion. Though she had finished all the food I'd made her eat this morning, she seemed as if she might collapse at any moment.

"Worry not," I told her. "We shall be safe soon."

She only gave me a grim smile and muttered something about having thought she'd be safe marrying Bluebeard. I tried to rub her back in a comforting way, but she flinched away from my touch.

I studied Franz's home while we waited. It was smaller, less grand, and less ancient than Bluebeard's castle, but still very fine. The house was built of red brick and clean lines, accented by white pillars and perfectly manicured shrubberies. Once I might have enjoyed imagining myself as mistress of these grounds, but now the things I wanted were both simpler and more vital, and I had no space for such dreams. I needed only to cure Liesl's fever. To find our way home. To live.

Franz, at last, hurried along the path to us, his guard lagging behind reluctantly. He looked handsome today, wearing a crisp emerald-green cravat with his usual all-black ensemble. His hair was styled in a pompadour, one curl falling across his high forehead. I smiled when I saw him, though I was also embarrassed at how disheveled I must appear, to have been taken for a beggar. I smoothed my hand over my hair and then wished I hadn't; my plaits were half undone, and the rain had made them frizzy.

"Herr Franz!" I said as he approached. "Thank goodness you are here. We need—"

"What are you doing here?" he hissed. His expression was usually solemn, so I hadn't thought it strange that he did not smile back at me, but his tone was so harsh when he spoke that I winced.

"We were . . . in danger," I said. "From Bluebeard. We had to run through the woods, and—" I was going to say that our brothers were on their way, but from the cold way Franz looked at me, I didn't want to share that information. "In any case," I said instead, "we need help."

"Bluebeard sent a letter," Franz said, in a tone so cold and distant that I hardly recognized it. "I know all about you and your sister's illness, your addled minds. I will take you in, but I must write to him so he can retrieve you."

"No!" I cried. "He'll kill us."

He raised an eyebrow. "I had hoped your sister was the more afflicted of you, but it seems you share her paranoia."

"Anne, we should go," Liesl whispered gently.

"My mind is not *addled*," I said, gritting my teeth. "The rumors of his past wives—of their disappearances—made it all the way to our village, so I am sure you have heard them, too."

He stiffened. "Wherever there is great wealth and eccentricity, there will be rumors. I will not interfere in another man's household affairs."

I pushed on, more from anger and stubbornness than any hope that he still might help us. "We know what happened to those other wives now. We cannot go back unless we wish to join them in death, tied to the castle and terrorizing whatever poor girl he takes as his next wife."

Liesl swooned, and I wrapped an arm around her to keep her upright. When I turned my attention back to Franz, he wore an expression of severe mistrust.

"You speak of ghosts, too," he said, shaking his head. "And to think I had once considered . . . "

My cheeks flamed. Why had I let slip a mention of the ghosts? He already thought us mad. I only wished we were, and that the things we had seen were not real. If I had not spent a whole morning washing blood out of my skirts, perhaps I would have been able to convince myself that we had imagined it all.

"I understand," I said. "I know it seems as if we speak nonsense and are terrified of our own shadows. And I know you have loyalties to him that have nothing to do with whatever you may have once felt for me." I spoke as clearly and calmly as I could, trying to fight anything he might interpret as evidence of "madness," even as my heart hammered against my ribs. "But please, can you help us? If only for a few hours so we can rest and warm ourselves by a fire?"

He shook his head slowly. "I cannot," he said. "If Bluebeard was to find out that I had harbored you . . ." Franz pressed his lips together and rubbed his neck. "He has offered a reward to whoever finds you, you know."

I drew myself up to my full height, which still meant tilting my head back to meet his eyes. Liesl's weight was still heavy on my shoulder, though she'd woken up again. "So you won't help us because you want the reward?"

"Of course not," Franz said, bristling. "But I do not suggest approaching other noblemen like this when there is so much for them to gain in returning Bluebeard's bride to him."

A tear streamed down Liesl's cheek, and I wiped it away.

"Thank you for your advice," I said, my words barbed.

"I am truly sorry I cannot do more," Franz said, and I thought perhaps he meant it, at least a little. It was the first time I'd seen anything that seemed like real sentiment on his face.

I swallowed. "Are you going to write and tell him we were here?"

His eyes flicked to Liesl, who was half-turned toward my shoulder, leaning on me, and he said, "As far as I'm concerned, this conversation never happened."

"Thank you," I said, letting out a relieved breath.

He took a few steps toward his grand house before he turned back and said, "Stay out of sight. And good luck, Fraulein Anne."

I thanked him again, more warmly this time. He was right, I suppose, and no one will be willing to help us. Gustav's estate is too far away to try, and even if it were not, what if we went all that way only to meet with the same response? Or worse, he might give us over to Bluebeard to gain the reward and his favor. Perhaps they never liked me at all, any of them, but saw in me an avenue to Bluebeard's wealth and influence.

So that is how Liesl and I ended up in the woods again, though at least we are farther from the castle than we were before and have some idea of where we are. Somehow, despite my aching ankle, I managed to help Liesl stumble along until we found a clearing in the woods. She is still feverish, but I hoped the sun might at least warm her and dry our clothes. Again, I turned to this journal. I shall run out of ink soon, but it is some small comfort to me while I have it.

Never in my life have I been so afraid. So hopeless. So alone.

Liesl is so ill that she can no longer help me decide what to do. Even if she were well, she is so downtrodden by what has happened that she no longer trusts her judgment. Oh, why did she not ask Klaus to go with her instead of me? He might have some idea of how to get out of this mess.

I am failing her.

And now I have smudged the ink. A tear fell onto the page, and when I wiped it away, I nearly ruined what I have written. But there is something else, too—there is a fox here.

It's sitting at the edge of the clearing, looking at us in the most unnatural way. It could not possibly be the same fox that led me to the hidden room, could it? And more impossible still, have the wives sent this fox to guide us?

Perhaps I am as mad as Franz thinks, as Bluebeard has told them I am.

I stood just now and the fox started to leave, but it stopped a few paces into the trees and turned as if to make sure I followed, just as it did at the castle. It may be madness, but I am going to wake Liesl and follow it. We cannot stay here much longer, and the fox's guidance seems as good as any. Let us hope it leads us somewhere safe, if anywhere can be safe for us now.

CHAPTER FORTY-THREE

Bluebeard's Diary | Rosalind

22 JANUARY, 21ST YEAR OF QUEEN THERESA I

Margaret's words come back to me often. Sometimes I feel they are all with me still, that their spirits have stayed with the castle, though of course, they would have no power over me. But perhaps they can watch as I spend the years that once belonged to them. I wonder what they think about the wives who came after them. Are they jealous that I may someday find one who will be strong enough to make the choice they could not? Who might be mine forever?

All these years of searching, and I found a wife better than them all. More loyal, more obedient. Even if they felt no envy for the others, they must have been jealous of Rosalind.

She was more beautiful, even, than Cacilie. Her skin was flawless, her cheekbones delicate, her hair the palest blonde, her mouth a perfect little rosebud. She moved gracefully and had impeccable manners. I believed I had finally found the perfect wife.

Rosalind had many suitors, but she never seemed to grow attached to any of them. I was not entirely sure whether she was attached to me, even after I courted her for months. She kept so much to herself, giving only faint smiles and mollifying answers whenever I tried to delve into her real feelings or thoughts. I suspected I might never truly know her, that I would never be her confidant. It was just as well; that was never what I wanted from her anyway.

But when I proposed, she said yes, and looked almost relieved. I had the strange sense that she was hiding from something, or that marriage to me would be an escape. Even if it was, I did not care. She executed her duties perfectly, growing more beautiful as her happiness grew in her marriage to me. She made me the envy of every man in Westenfall.

Her favorite thing of all was to spend hours in the garden, often with her lady's maid, Idonia. I have never seen a noblewoman take such a liking or pursue such a friendship with one not of her class. It did not bother me, since she seemed so happy, laughing as she spent time with Idonia in the flower garden she designed for the eastern hill. When she hosted events at my castle, Idonia kept herself away, so it wasn't as if anyone but I would notice Rosalind's friendship with someone below her station.

Rosalind was perfect, and I waited several years to test her. She was the most beautiful woman I had ever seen in my life, and I might never see another of her caliber again. I dreaded losing her, dreaded having to wait years before trying again with someone new if she failed. I had no need for the years she had left, having taken so many for myself from the wives before her. She never disobeyed me or declined to do anything I asked of her in all that time, so I told myself she was the one who would finally pass. Who would not use the key.

But of course, she failed, and I had to deal with her as I had all the others.

I begin to feel like Sisyphus, forever rolling a rock uphill, only for it to come crashing down again whenever I near the peak. I am thoroughly discouraged now, but I am sure in some matter of years, I shall rise to the challenge and try again.

CHAPTER FORTY-FOUR

Anne's Diary

16 OCTOBER

So much has happened, but I shall pick up first where I left off.

I hauled Liesl to her feet, and she leaned her weight on me, her cheek burning my shoulder from her fever. Though I stumbled on slowly, trying to navigate the pair of us through the trees and undergrowth with my one good ankle, the fox never got so far ahead that it was out of sight. It really felt as if it was leading us, and I am still unsure whether that fox was truly there, or if I so needed a guide at that moment that my mind conjured one for me.

In any case, real or imagined, the fox led us to Hugo.

We reached the edge of the woods and stepped out into the fading sunlight over a green pasture full of grazing sheep. Liesl mumbled incoherently; I do not think she knew whether she was asleep or awake. Dragging her through the forest had taken its toll on me. I collapsed, Liesl falling half on top of me, and I wasn't sure whether I could rise again. The smell of the pasture—the damp earth and the fall wildflowers—ached like home, and for a moment, I closed my eyes and breathed it in. When I opened my eyes, the fox was gone.

As I looked around for it, a young man approached us. He carried a shepherd's crook and wore simple clothing that stretched tight over his broad shoulders. Sandy hair fell over his brow, which was furrowed in an expression of cautious concern.

With great effort, I sat up and tried to wake Liesl. She only moaned and rolled over. "I am sorry," I told the shepherd boy. "We do not mean to trespass."

He stopped and glanced between Liesl and me. "Are you in need of a place to stay?"

The way he said it—so kindly, so simply—made me want to cry. Such a contrast from my morning conversation with Franz. "Yes," I whispered as I staggered to my feet.

He only nodded and then scooped Liesl up in his arms as easily as if she were a newborn lamb in the spring. I followed him to the edge of the pasture and up a hill, finding some reserve of strength within me now that I had hope of a fire and somewhere indoors to rest. At the top of the hill, I saw where he was taking us—a little cottage like the one we'd grown up in, with a plume of smoke spouting from the chimney.

Again, I felt that if I were not so exhausted, I would cry.

Inside the house, we were greeted by a tall, sandy-haired woman who must have been his mother. She reminded me a little of Cook—the sort of person who makes you feel warm and safe.

Though their bare cupboards showed what little they had to share, she only asked her son, "What have you brought me?"

"They were in the meadow," he said as he laid Liesl gently on what must be his mother's bed and tucked a covered quilt over her. "She's feverish."

"I'm Minna," the woman said to me. "And this is my son, Hugo."

"I'm—" I stopped. Introducing myself could put them at risk if anyone came looking for us. I picked the first name that came to mind instead. "I'm Amalie," I said. "And this is my sister, Margaret."

"Amalie?" Minna asked as if she did not believe me.

I only nodded, unsure whether I had the strength to fabricate further lies. She studied me a few moments longer but did not push for more details. "Well, Amalie, you and your sister are welcome to stay here for as long as you need."

She sat on the bed beside Liesl and smoothed a hand over her forehead. "Get me some willow bark for tea," she said. Hugo put the kettle on the fire and hurried out the door to do as she asked.

Feeling useless, I stepped closer to the bed. "Will she be alright?" I asked, my voice trembling.

"Yes," Minna said. "We just need to break her fever. Now, help me get her out of these damp clothes."

I did as she asked, appreciating Minna's confidence and calm, steady hands. I was boundlessly grateful that she asked us no more questions about how we came to be there. After Liesl was stripped down to her undergarments and tucked under a couple of blankets, I changed out of mine, too, and wrapped myself in a quilt beside the hearth while Minna hung our dresses on the line outside to dry.

Before long, Hugo came in with the bark, and Minna made two cups of tea.

She handed me the first, and I thanked her, appreciating the way it warmed my hands. I sipped the tea and winced a little at the bitter taste.

"I'm sorry," Minna said. "We have no honey." She sat beside Liesl again, holding the other cup and gently nudging her. I held my breath until Liesl blinked awake. She frowned as her eyes focused on Minna, then looked wildly around the room until she saw me.

"I'm here," I said. "All is well. Drink the tea; it will help your fever."

She sat up against the wall, Minna helping her, and sipped from the carved wooden cup. Once she started, she gulped down the rest quickly. I am sure she was as dehydrated as I had been, our wineskin long run dry. I'd nearly forgotten about Hugo, but he sat quietly in the corner, whittling a piece of wood.

I felt so much in their debt already, but I had nothing I could give them. After what Franz had told me about the letters Bluebeard sent out, perhaps the best gift we could give them would be to leave as soon as possible. I vowed that the moment Liesl was in any state to travel, we would. Until then, I decided to offer them what little of the truth seemed safe to tell them.

"I cannot thank you both enough for taking us in," I said. "We were in danger where we were, and had to run. We became lost in the woods, and it rained and . . . and then Hugo found us."

Minna gave me that long, knowing look, as if she saw everything else that I wasn't telling. Liesl's eyes had slipped closed again, and

Minna finally turned away to help her lie down in the bed once more.

Remembering my satchel, I pulled out the bread and apples that were left. "We have little with us, but please, I want you to have it."

Only after I'd taken out the food did I realize the mistake I'd made. The apples would raise no questions, but the bread was not the sort two peasant girls should have. They were delicate, airy breads that valued flavor over heartiness. The kind Cook would not let me help make because mine always turned out rough and mealy.

Minna again said nothing, though I knew she saw them and understood what they meant. She took them from me and placed them on their small table before the hearth. "We shall have these with dinner."

"Thank you," I said. "As soon as Li–Margaret is better we shall be on our way." I blushed at my slip, but Minna either didn't notice or decided to pretend she hadn't. I suspect she already knew they were not our true names anyhow.

"Where will you be on your way to?" she asked, gently pushing a sweaty lock of Liesl's hair back from her brow. It struck me that I should be the one tending to Liesl, but I still felt weak down to my bones, though the hearth fire and the willow-bark tea were helping.

And then her words sank in, and a new wave of panic flooded me. Where could I tell her we were going when I did not even know? I obviously could not mention Bluebeard's castle, but was saying Coesfeld any safer? And I certainly could not say the truth—that we would be going back to wandering the woods.

"I only ask," Minna said, "because Hugo is to go into Herford to sell some of our spun and dyed wool at the market tomorrow. If your way lies in that direction, perhaps he could escort you there."

"Yes, thank you. If he could escort us as far as Herford, that would be wonderful," I said, though I'd never heard of such a place and could only hope it took us farther from Bluebeard. "We could not ask for more."

Minna sent Hugo away again on some errand, then gave me her other dress to wear so I would not have to stay wrapped in the quilt until my clothing dried. She insisted I lie in bed next to Liesl and sleep, and I was too weary to refuse.

When I woke, it was dark outside, and the smell of stew filled the cottage. Our dresses had been brought inside and lay folded at the foot of the bed. I felt better than I had since before we discovered that awful room.

After changing into my own dress again and eating two hearty bowls of stew while trying to make conversation with Hugo, who seems rather shy and keenly worried about Liesl, I asked if they had any ink. Right after asking, I regretted it, afraid I'd offended them. Many of our class do not read and write. But they did have some ink, though as I am sure you can see, it is made from wood ash and so not as smooth as the ink I once used at the castle.

Then I sat at the table and wrote this by the light of one of the candles from my satchel until long after Minna and Hugo had gone to sleep in the other small room of the cottage. It has helped to record all that has happened, and I am especially touched by the kindness of Minna and Hugo and even the washerwoman near Franz's village.

Hope seems a dangerous thing to have under the circumstances, but I will admit I now believe there is a chance that our brothers will arrive before Bluebeard finds us. I pray God keeps them safe and allows them to easily defeat Liesl's wretched husband. Though I remember his display of swordsmanship back in Coesfeld, how he defeated all the other noblemen, and my stomach hurts with hopelessness.

Now that Liesl and I are safe—for however short a time—I can feel more than just horror and panic at what we witnessed. I think of those wives, their bodies hung in the dark below the castle, their spirits haunting the halls, and I weep.

Did they love Bluebeard? When did they discover that he was not a man but a wolf hidden in velvet and smiles? Perhaps it was only in the moment before their lives bled away that they saw this. Or were there hints, as time went on in their marriages, that he was not as he seemed? That he'd lined them up like lambs for slaughter?

Perhaps they were all like us: foolish and so grateful for his favor that we could not see what they tried to show us. For surely that was why they kept Liesl awake at night.

They wanted to warn her, as they had not been warned.

I weep also for myself. Or rather, for the girl I was. A girl who dreamt of castles, her dress torn and muddied from tending goats. A girl who did not know what harm wishes may bring, who had never stepped in another's blood . . .

That girl is gone now. There are things that can't be unseen or unknown. I now must twist myself into something stronger to survive in this world which is so much worse I thought it was.

CHAPTER FORTY-FIVE

Letter from Klaus

16 OCTOBER

Anne,

We are coming as quickly as we can and have brought some friends from the village with us. However, travel has been impeded by the storm, and we did not have the money to hire horses for the journey. All the rain has made the streams along our path swell so much they're near impossible to cross. We're making our way to you as swiftly as we can. God willing, it shall only take two more days.

I have hired someone to deliver this letter, and he has promised to place it in no one's hands but yours, lest it should endanger you further with Bluebeard. I pray our messenger finds you alive and well, and that this has all been a misunderstanding.

With love and worry,
Klaus

CHAPTER FORTY-SIX

Anne's Diary

17 OCTOBER

This morning, Liesl's fever broke. She looked more awake and healthier than I had seen her in a long time. I hugged her tightly, and Minna excused herself from the house to give us some time alone. Hugo was already out tending to the sheep.

"I'm relieved you are well again," I told Liesl. "I was so worried for you."

Liesl embraced me back, and the strength in her arms sent another wave of relief through me. She began to weep as I held her. "Oh Anne, I'm so sorry."

"Hush, Liesl, there is nothing to be sorry for."

She pulled away and wiped her eyes. "Yes, there is. We would be in no danger if I had not been so selfish as to marry him."

I placed my hand on her knee. "I know you did so to protect our family. You told me as much; that we would never go hungry again. It was an incredible, selfless thing that you did."

She shook her head, more tears falling. "That is what I told you and what I told myself, too. But I did it for me, Anne. Do you not see? I hated our life before."

My mouth fell open in surprise. I had never suspected Liesl was unhappy at home.

"Those fairy tales we used to tell each other . . . " Liesl sniffed and pulled her knees to her chest. "I wanted that for myself. Not the power of true love to transform—I knew I had no love for Bluebeard, and though I did not know what sort of monster he was, I never expected I would change him. No, what I always wanted from those tales was an easy life."

"Who doesn't dream of that sometimes? You're being too hard on yourself."

Liesl shook her head. "Not only sometimes. All the time. Remember when the butcher's boy proposed to me a couple of years ago? I think perhaps I could have been content with him, but I wanted more, and I knew he would never do more than become the village butcher like his father. When Bluebeard came and wanted to marry me, I thought it was proof that I had been right to refuse him, that I was destined for more." She wiped tears away, looking angry now. "Look at the mess I made, all because I wanted more than I was born to. We could be caught and killed, our father and brothers might be hurt too if they try to save us . . . "

"Don't be so hard on yourself," I said. "No one can blame you for acting in your own interest, as well as in your family's."

"I can, and I do blame myself. You might be safe at home still—we both would be safe at home—if not for me."

"I might have said yes to Bluebeard if you denied him," I said, but it didn't sound convincing even to my own ears. All this time, I had thought Liesl was making a sacrifice I was not capable of, and now I see that she had believed herself sacrificing her old life for a better one.

She gave me a bitter smile. "It would be better if we had never met him. Or at least, if I had not asked you to come with me."

I comforted her the best I could, telling her that all would work out for the best in the end, though I do not yet believe it myself.

I have thought about it more since, and I confess I still am not sure if it truly would have been better never to have met the man. We would not know what we had missed, so perhaps we should have been better off had he never spotted us in the meadow. But I also have a whole treasury of memories, now, from my time living in Bluebeard's castle. We were able to see and do so many more things than we had even dreamt of in our meadow.

Of course, some of those memories are now steeped in bitterness. I was so happy for most of the time I spent with Sebastian. And yet all along, he knew. He knew, and he continued to work for that monster of a man. He did nothing but give me cryptic half-warnings and bid me leave the castle. How can I reconcile that with the boy who had seemed so kind, who wanted only to fill the castle and its grounds with life?

"We cannot change the past," I said. "But even if I could, I would still go with you. I would not allow you to go through this alone, even if it does not end well."

"The garden," Liesl said, as if she'd just remembered it. "The one on the hill, where you hid the food. Is that what you worked on for so long with Sebastian?"

"Yes," I said, stiffening at the remembrance. "I wanted to show you. I restored it at least partly for you, but you were so ill."

She waved a hand distractedly. "It is only that you spent so much time with him." I said nothing, carefully gazing at a spot on the wall. "I had suspected that you might . . . be growing to care for him."

I swallowed. "Perhaps I did. Perhaps our whole family are terrible judges of people," I said, forcing a laugh that sounded more like a cough.

"Why do you say that? He seemed kind enough. And quite a capable gardener."

"Just as I thought Franz was," I said, shaking my head. Something stopped me from telling her of Sebastian's warnings. I did not want her to think ill of him, even if I did now. "And yet he would not help us. And Sebastian—he must know what goes on in that castle, what Bluebeard—"

Liesl winced when I said his name, so I stopped. She recovered, though, and placed a hand on her knee. "His last wife was many years ago. Sebastian must have been a small child then. He could not have known."

Except he had known *something*. Why else would he have warned me, had said it was not safe for me there, was already too late for

Liesl? But I felt far too guilty to tell Liesl that, so I said only, "Do you think any of the other servants knew? Idonia must have, she has been there so long."

"If they did, how could they stay in his service?"

That sounded like something I would have thought before our whole ordeal, but now I feel wiser, or perhaps only more bitter. Liesl married a man she did not love for a better life. Surely there are others who would go further, who would do much more for a comfortable life in the castle, even the life of a servant.

"Idonia warned me away from the room beneath the castle," I reminded her.

"That shows that she knows it's forbidden," Liesl said. "It does not prove she knows why." I was not convinced, but she said, more softly, "She was kind to me. I do not want to think poorly of her unless I know there is good reason I should."

I could also have told her of the poison garden then. Perhaps I should have done so as soon as I discovered it, but would it have changed anything? And what would it help now? "Very well," I said. "I shall try to believe that none of the castle servants knew what he did."

"Such horrible things," Liesl whispered. "I wish I could forget them or persuade myself they were not real."

Her eyes grew glassy again, and I wrapped my arms around her. She hugged me back, and I knew then that, though we could not see it yet, there must be a way out of this. I would find it. I would save us both.

"Girls?" Minna asked, and we pulled apart.

"Yes?" Liesl asked.

Minna handed us each a bowl of porridge and sat on the end of the bed. "Eat," she said. "You need your strength."

We obeyed. I wanted to object to how much of her food and kindness Minna had shared with us—it was more than we could ever hope to repay—but my stomach overcame my pride. Minna sat with us as we ate, chewing her thumbnail and seeming as if she wanted to tell us something but had not yet found the right words.

Liesl must have picked up on it, too. When she'd finished her breakfast, she wiped her mouth on her sleeve and set the bowl on her nightstand. "What is it, Minna?"

Minna took a deep breath and exhaled slowly before beginning. "I took you in, not just because you needed help and it was the right thing to do, but because I feel guilty."

I sat up straighter, now afraid of what Minna might have to feel guilty about. Was everyone we met to have a sordid past and dangerous secrets?

"A long time ago," Minna said, "I once lived at Tiefenwald Castle."

Liesl and I both gasped and looked at each other, eyes wide.

"Yes," she said. "I deduced you girls came from there."

"You're Amalie," I said. "You escaped."

She smiled grimly and shook her head. "No, but the names you used—Margaret and Amalie—were two of his former wives. I served as Amalie's lady's maid, which is how I came to live in the castle. And besides that, I saw the fear in your eyes, and the circumstances

. . . After the horrid things that happened to me there, I was able to guess what happened to you."

"Then you know those are not our real names. I am sorry, but I thought if we told you, it could endanger you. My name is—"

"All is well," she said. "You were right to be cautious—there is no need to tell me your true names." Minna went on without looking at us. "Amalie brought me with her when she was married to him. We spent several happy months together in the castle before things began to sour. My lady had great trouble sleeping, and when I spent a night in her chambers, I understood why: she was being haunted."

Liesl and I exchanged a glance, and she said, "I, too, spent many sleepless nights in the castle because of these 'hauntings.' It was the past wives, wasn't it? Trying to warn us."

Minna nodded. "Yes," she said. "At the time, I did not know. I didn't even know Bluebeard had had other wives. But now, I believe I might know more about what has happened in that castle than almost anyone. Well, anyone still alive."

"What sort of things happened in your lady's room?" I asked, then worried it was a macabre question. But I had struggled to believe any of it was real, and now we'd found someone who had experienced it, too, who knew even more than we did.

"The doors and windows opened on their own, candles sputtered out and relit themselves," Minna said. "Books fell from shelves. I'm guessing that was his fourth wife, Margaret. Singing and piano notes from his second wife, Renate."

"Was there a fox?" I asked, and when she nodded, I felt such relief that I had not imagined that either.

"Yes, that would have been Thekla. From what I know of her, she spent her days in the forest and loved all the woodland creatures, so it made sense that she might use one of them."

"And the roses and other flowers," Liesl said. "Who was that?" Her eyes widened, and she leaned toward Minna, as enthralled as I was.

Minna grimaced. "Flowers could have been from Rosalind, though there were few at the castle in her time. Roses were Amalie's favorite flower—I still have handkerchiefs she stitched with them. She planted a great number of colorful rosebushes in her own little square of the garden. I suppose if you saw or smelled roses, that was a message from her."

I inhaled sharply. So, she was gone, too. One of the bodies we had seen . . . A little spark of hope within me extinguished.

"I am so sorry," Liesl said, her eyes shiny.

The older woman pressed her lips together and nodded. "I could not save her. We did not learn soon enough what had become of the others, so when it came her time . . . it was too late."

"We know so little still," I said. "Except what became of his other wives."

"What I do not understand," Liesl said, "is why he gave me the golden key at all? If he had not, I might never have found them, might never have connected their deaths with the strange things we experienced within the castle."

"It is a test, or at least that is how he thinks of it. He has always been looking for an obedient wife, one who is not curious about what shall become of her when he needs to extend his life again."

"Extend his life?" I asked, my brow furrowing.

"It is not just in revenge for their disobedience that he kills them," Minna said slowly. "He uses their blood—their lives—for dark, forbidden magic. That is how he has survived for over one hundred years."

My jaw fell open, and I looked at Liesl in shocked silence. Surely, he could not have lived so long. It was not possible, and even less possible that he should still look younger than our father.

"I did not believe it at first either," Minna said. "But then I saw the corpses of his wives in the dungeons and the scrolls describing them. I learned how impossible it is to kill him."

"How do you know all this?" Liesl asked.

At the same time, I said, "Impossible to kill—does that mean you tried?"

"The answer to both your questions is Idonia, the housekeeper. Does she live? Is she still there?"

Liesl and I nodded.

"I am glad to hear it. She told me all this," Minna said. "And it is she who has tried to kill him for years. I helped, but it did not matter. All the risks he took . . . he was often injured, but never died. Idonia has seen him gored by boar and stag alike on his hunts, stabbed in a tavern brawl. Once he even fell from the castle rooftop. And yet he lives. He is not of this world, and cannot be killed as other mortals are."

Another long silence hung heavy in the air, punctuated only by the crackling of the fire in the hearth. Her words were ominous, and before living in that accursed castle, I would not have believed them.

But now, after what we had seen, I did. I believed them even as I wanted them to be untrue. For if he could not be killed, our brothers could not save us and were themselves in grave danger.

"But Idonia," I said. "She has been with the castle so long. She knows what he has done, and she has been trying to kill him? Oh—the poison garden!"

"What?" Liesl asked, breathless, and I winced, feeling guilty.

"She has a whole garden of poisons," I explained quickly. "I discovered it, but I did not want to tell you because you already seemed so unwell . . . and I even thought Idonia might be making you ill." I stared at my hands. "That's why I began to prepare our afternoon tea."

"Oh," Liesl said, her hand going to her heart. "How could you not tell me?"

"I'm sorry," I said. "But you trusted her, and you already seemed so lonely. I did not want to take away another friend. Besides, I had no proof, and after the fox, I was afraid I might be going mad. Either way, it was foolish—I mistrusted Idonia when all along it was Bluebeard."

"I do not blame you for that," Minna said. "I also distrusted Idonia at first. All these years of foiled plans have made her rather cold and harsh. And I imagine if I had been in her role—had seen several wives go through the castle, served them, and seen them killed—I would not be as strong as she is now."

"So she does know," I said, feeling sick. How could she serve such a monster?

"Yes," Minna said. "She was the dear friend of the fifth wife, Rosalind, and came to the castle with her. After my lady was killed, Idonia told me everything she knew. She and the gardener helped me flee the castle. She had nowhere to go when Rosalind was killed and instead pretended to believe Bluebeard's story about his young wife running away so she could stay on as the housekeeper. There is more to her story, but it is not mine to tell."

I'd been curious about Idonia many times since we came to the castle—especially after finding her poison garden—but now I wanted to know everything about her. Perhaps if I had tried to get to know her, she might have taken me into her confidence as she had Minna. She had tried to warn me away from the room beneath the castle—perhaps she might have told me why, and we would not be here now. All because I was too stubborn and angry and suspicious of her.

"What did you do?" Liesl asked. "I mean, after you left."

Minna leaned back in her simple wooden chair. "I lived in great fear for several years that Bluebeard would come after me. But perhaps he never found out what I knew, or Idonia lied for me, or a lady's maid was not worth the trouble to track down and dispatch. Whatever the reason, I never heard from him again. In time I met my husband—God rest his soul—and we were able to build this farm together. As a widower, he knew sorrow himself, and could understand mine. Hugo was only a little boy then, and I have raised him as my own."

"Thank you," I said. "For taking us in when you must know the danger it could bring to your home."

"Do not thank me," Minna said, straightening and raising her chin. "As I said, I took you in because I have felt guilty all these years. How many wives, I wondered, has he taken since? With all I know, I should have found a way to stop him. But I was afraid, first for myself and then of leaving Hugo motherless again. But he is grown now, and this is only a small thing, but I pray it will help atone for all the things I did not do."

Liesl leaned forward from her place on the bed and took Minna's hands in hers. "I am the only wife since your Amalie. You have wronged no one. And you said yourself, he is no ordinary mortal."

"He may not be mortal as we are," I said, "but there must be some way—he cannot be all-powerful."

Liesl caught my eyes, biting her lip. She knew I was thinking of our brothers. Had we led them into a trap, a fight with an unkillable monster?

"Idonia has tried many different combinations and strengths of poisons in his tea, but he is immune to them all. He fully recovers from any injury by the next morning. And yet he looks like any other man, except for one thing."

"His blue beard," I said.

"The blue sheen is subtle," Minna admitted. "But it grows with the years even as the rest of him remains unchanging. Could that be a mark of his deal with the devil? His work in dark magic? I do not know." She drummed her fingers on the table. "But I suppose it does not matter. I will never return, and I hope you shall not either."

"We must. Our brothers are coming to rescue us, and now we know they shall not be able to defeat him." I shook my head. "At the very least, we must try to intercept our brothers before they reach Tiefenwald Castle. We need to stop them. After that, I don't know what we shall do."

"We have endangered you long enough," Liesl said, attempting to get out of bed. She stood but then sat back down quickly. "I am a little dizzy still. But never mind that, I shall be ready to journey on soon."

Minna tucked her back into bed somewhat forcefully. "I will not allow you to leave until you can at least walk on your own. Rest, child. Perhaps tomorrow you shall have strength enough for a journey. Though I'd rather you not undertake such a journey at all. Hugo has delayed his trip to Herford—he can take you in that direction tomorrow if you change your mind."

Reluctantly, Liesl relented and quickly fell back into a deep slumber. I borrowed more ink to record all Minna told us. I pray God will bless her for all her kindness to us and that she will have peace, despite all that she saw in that dreadful castle. I agree with her that Liesl is in no state for a journey, but I also pray she shall recover soon. We must warn our brothers, and I am afraid we do not have the day to waste.

CHAPTER FORTY-SEVEN

Letter from Liesl

17 OCTOBER

Dearest Mother,

Anne and I are safe, for now. A woman named Minna—lady's maid to the wife before me—and her kind son have taken us in. I was too feverish to recall how we came to safety, but I have a brief memory of being carried in strong arms and the warmth of their home washing over me as we passed through the door.

Anne says a fox sent by the ghosts of the slain wives led us here, and after all I have experienced since my wedding, I believe it. Anne and Minna believe their spirits were trying to show me the truth and give me the chance to run, to save myself and Anne. But I cannot help but feel that they wanted more from me, something darker. Vengeance for what was taken from them. After all, had they not led us to their blood-soaked room, I would still be ignorant and safe.

I shudder to think how close we came to joining them. I might still end with a hook through me, my blood spilled to lengthen the life of a monster. Perhaps I, too, will want retribution, and will haunt his next victims until I have it.

And yet, when I think of my husband, there is something besides hate. An unsettling feeling which I dare not share, even with Anne. I hate what he has done and fear him, of course. But there is also the desire to understand. Why has he done all of this? Why did someone who has made himself so far beyond a mortal man choose me as his wife? And why was he so eager for Anne to join me?

When we spoke before he left, why did he seem touched that I wanted to know him better? Why was he ever sweet to me if all along he had planned to kill me?

I do not know what will happen next, or if we will find a way to escape to safety, but I miss you more than words can say. We shall rely on your continued assistance from the afterlife. I can only guess that is how we have made it this far.

With all my love,

Liesl

CHAPTER FORTY-EIGHT

Bluebeard's Diary | Amalie

23 APRIL, 9TH YEAR OF KING LUKAS IV

S he escaped me.

Things had gone so well with Amalie that I had not even bothered to write of her until today. And now, she is gone.

Knowing I might not find another beauty like Cacilie or Rosalind or a wild spirit like Thekla, I had decided this time to look for another shy, meek woman like Margaret. Amalie was pretty enough, though nothing out of the ordinary, and so shy that it was hard for her to even keep her eyes on me for the proposal.

A dreamy little thing, she spent her days in my castle embroidering handkerchiefs and having the gardener plant as many rose bushes as he could. She did not enjoy playing hostess at my events or trying to command the castle staff, but I have Idonia to look after those things now, so it did not matter. Unlike Rosalind or Thekla, I believed Amalie might truly love me.

She asked me questions about my past, and I decided to answer them. I told her of the other wives—what they were like, the false stories of how they died—only playing with the dates so she would not realize how old I am. "Oh, you poor man," she used to say. "You've been through so much pain, such tragedy."

I was the brooding widower once again, she the delicate new light in my life, and that worked for us. For years, even.

My five past failures weighed on me, and I worried that by testing her, I would ruin something good once again. I have come to think of myself like Hades, looking for a Persephone to join me by my side. But even if they would not pursue immortality, how can I accept a partner afraid of the darkness within me? If I could not have one who would become like me, I must have one that sees no darkness in me at all. One who, even when given the opportunity, would not look for a different version of my past than the one I gave her.

So I tested Amalie, and of course, she was found just as disobedient and untrustworthy as all the others. Worse still, before I could get her down to the altar in my dungeon, she escaped me and ran into the night. It is storming, and she is such a frail little thing that I doubt she shall last until the morning. But still, if anyone should find her before I do, the things she knows could destroy me. I would surely be punished in the afterlife, if my demise ever should come, so I must see that the one thing that may defeat me is never found out.

I comfort myself that, whatever my errant wife says to anyone, I have the influence and wealth and skills to repair my reputation. But my heart is broken at her failure, and I hunger for the years she took with her when she fled.

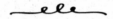

Two Days Later

I found Amalie before anyone else could. She has been taken care of like the rest. The lion's share of six lives now courses through my veins, giving me youth and vitality for centuries to come. I have land and wealth and status, so much that despite my long years, I still do not grow tired of it all. I do not need a wife. Six outstanding women have been tested, and none have been found worthy of me. I am taking a vow not to try again, to give up on my dream of sharing my rich, immortal life with another.

CHAPTER FORTY-NINE

Anne's Diary

18 OCTOBER

This morning at breakfast, Liesl was out with Minna proving that she could walk, at least a little, and I was finally able to thank Hugo for finding us and bringing us to their home. I had not seen him alone since he first spotted us and carried Liesl here.

"I am so happy that it led us to you," I said after explaining about the fox. "I cannot thank you enough for all you and your mother have done. Had you not brought us home, I am not sure we would still be alive. Especially my sister."

"There is no need for thanks," he said. "Do you think she will be well now?" He ran a hand over his forehead.

"Her health is much better." I wanted to comfort him, as there was something wholesome and endearing about him, and I did not want to lie, but of course, I did not know if either of us would be well, with a horrible man after us and our brothers in danger. And even if we did somehow survive, would we ever be "well" again, or would we be haunted by ghosts and nightmares whether waking or asleep?

"I am glad to hear it," he said, and his shoulders relaxed. "I was so worried, but especially for her. Do you think . . . do you think she might come to the pasture with me today? And you may come too of course," he added hastily.

"The exercise might do her good."

"And the sun and fresh air," he added.

"You should take her, then, if she wants to go," I said. Perhaps Liesl would like to take a moment to thank her rescuer as I had just done, though he did not seem comfortable accepting thanks. "I am going to stay here to help your mother."

Really, she was helping me, for she showed me how to spin wool expertly and gave me some of her dye recipes. It seems our debt to this family only grows, and we shall never be able to repay it, even if we do live past these next few days.

Liesl was happy to go with Hugo when he took the sheep out to pasture, though she seemed a little tired from her first walk with Minna. We have resolved to leave after lunchtime today. On foot, and without all our nighttime wanderings in the forest, we think it shall take us walking all today and through the night to reach the road to the castle. I pray that is fast enough to intercept our brothers and flee this land together.

I thanked Minna when we had finished with the wool, and she was just as hesitant to accept any thanks as her son had been.

"If I were truly brave," she said, "I would go with you to the castle. I would find a way to end Bluebeard's life once and for all. But I have spent so long being afraid that I no longer know another way. Please," she said, placing a hand lightly on my shoulder, "do not let yourself become like me. Fear is no way to live."

"You're too hard on yourself. You survived, and that alone wasn't easy," I said, because it was true and because I could make her no such promise. Every time I think of returning, I shudder, and if my love for our brothers was any less, I would run far from the castle as fast as I could.

I've just finished sewing the two daggers I have left—the third was so mangled from cutting branches that I gave it to Minna, hoping she can sell the jewels—into my plain gardening dress. It is near lunchtime, and so I must end here. If I am able, I will update again once we arrive at the castle, though there is a long day and night ahead of us. I pray Liesl's new strength will hold.

As it turned out, Liesl's strength did not need to hold for long. Only a couple of leagues from Minna's farm, we heard two men on horseback coming up the road. We dashed into the woods, hoping to avoid being seen. We were, though. I heard the men shout to each other. Noblemen, I ascertained, as I made out their clothing through gaps in the ferns and undergrowth in which we crouched. They'd seen us and were moving toward us.

Liesl grabbed my hand, trying to pull me deeper into the forest, but I was frozen in place. Because I'd recognized one of the men. Gustav.

"I saw them, Father," he said, standing not a stone's throw away from me as he scanned the woods. "Anne!" he called. "Fraulein Anne, are you there?"

Liesl stopped pulling at my hand and met my eyes, hers wide. Her expression asked me if I trusted him. Before my visit to Herr Franz's estate, I would have said "yes." Now, I shook my head. I didn't know.

Gustav's father went to his side, and they both moved closer to the woods. I was frozen. This boy had written me a poem. He felt *something* for me. Maybe he could help. Maybe they could take us on horseback to the road, and we could find our brothers in time, and everything would be well again.

"Fraulein Anne!" Gustav called again. "We're here to help you and your sister. Please come out."

That settled it. I stood up, dragging Liesl with me. "Herr Gustav," I said, doing my best to curtsy, though my skirts snagged in the undergrowth.

"You're alive!" Gustav said, smiling in his merry way. "Everyone's been so worried."

"Come," his father said. "Let's get you safely back to the castle."

"We cannot go back," I said sharply. "Bluebeard will hurt my sister. He already tried to kill her." My conversation with Franz weighed all too heavily on my mind, and I was careful to say nothing of ghosts, nothing to make them think we had lost our wits.

Gustav and his father exchanged a glance. "That is unfortunate," his father said steadily. "If that be the case, we certainly cannot take you back to him. At least, not until these accusations are proven unfounded."

Liesl stepped forward and said, "We need to intercept our brothers where the road to Tiefenwald Castle splits from the main thoroughfare. They will help us, but I fear that if they reach Bluebeard before we do, there will be violence."

Another long glance between him and Gustav, and he said, "Very well. We shall, of course, take you ladies wherever you need to go."

Liesl squeezed my hand once, then allowed the older nobleman to help her onto the back of his horse. Gustav helped me onto his. If I were not so terrified, perhaps I might have felt a spark at the touch of his hand or a flutter in my belly when he urged me to lean close and hang onto him as he urged his horse to a trot. The sort of thing I had felt before, all those times we'd danced together.

We are taking a break now to rest the horses. I thought it best to write a little something while we were here. Lest anything should happen, I would want everyone to know who our rescuers were.

I have the strangest feeling. It is like waking up from a nightmare, in those moments when you are still not quite sure what is real and what is dream. But we are drawing nearer the thoroughfare. We can await our brothers along the road, and they will help us from there.

Chapter Fifty

Anne's Diary

18 October

Yet again, I have been foolish and naïve and trusted when I should have doubted. And now Liesl and I shall both pay for it.

Gustav and his father did not take us to the road, as we asked, but instead directly to the castle. When the road became familiar and I realized where we were, I said to Gustav, "Wait, we should be heading east. Turn back."

He said nothing, and my stomach sank like an anchor. I called out to Liesl, then jumped from the horse, rolling and running toward the shadowy woods. Gustav was on me, tackling me to the ground in a way that told me he no longer saw me as someone to be courted or a dancing partner or even a lady. No, I was only reward money to him now.

I looked up to Liesl from where my face was pressed into the damp earth. She hadn't escaped either, hadn't even made it off the horse. Gustav's father held her in a vice-like grip.

A sudden, dark impulse flared within me. The weight of the daggers sewn into my sleeve pressed heavy against my arm, and I was tempted to pull one out and stab Gustav.

That was what finally made me stop struggling, what allowed him to wordlessly put me back on his horse, in front of him this time, so his arms encircled me like a cage. Gustav might have been signing our death warrants, but he did not know that, and he didn't deserve to die for it.

Besides, I must save the two daggers I have left for my true target. It will do me no good if Bluebeard suspects that I am armed and searches me.

It was near nightfall by the time we were back in the Great Hall of the castle, in Idonia's custody. Gustav and his father took their reward and left without so much as a guilty glance toward us. There was but one small relief: Bluebeard was still out hunting for us.

As Idonia, straight-backed and stone-faced as ever, shut the door behind our captors, I turned to apologize to Liesl. But before I could get any words out, Idonia whirled on us.

"My girls, you're safe!" she cried, crushing us to her with warm, strong arms. When she pulled away, her eyes were wet with tears.

Liesl and I exchanged an incredulous glance. We'd learned a little of her past from Minna, but nothing that would make us expect her to show affection for us like this.

"We are not safe at all," Liesl said. "My husband returns soon—you said so yourself."

Idonia wiped her eyes with her handkerchief. "Yes, of course, you have not escaped him yet. But I was worried sick for you, out on your own in the woods."

I wondered if she remembered Minna, if it was safe to tell her that Minna had helped us. But it was only in the last few days that I had learned enough about Idonia to trust her, and Minna had done far too much for us to dare anything that might cause her harm.

"We must prepare you to flee again," Idonia said.

Liesl shook her head. "We have nowhere to run."

"And Bluebeard will know we were returned—he'll kill you if he learns you helped us get away again," I said.

Idonia waved a hand. "I have had a long life, full of many failures. I will do right by you, though it may be the last thing I do."

"No," Liesl said. "I have a plan."

I turned to her. "What kind of plan?" I did not like that it didn't seem to involve running away from this godforsaken place.

"Trust me," Liesl said, as if I had any other choice.

"Whatever you have in mind," Idonia said, "it will not work. I have been slowly poisoning him for longer than both your lives added together, and yet he lives."

Belatedly, I remembered to act surprised at this, not wanting to give away that we had been with Minna.

"My plan will work," Liesl said with more confidence than she had shown in a long time. "I understand him, in a way. He will still want me, even after all of this. If I say the right things . . . "

I gasped. "You can't be serious, Liesl."

"I am. He wants a wife who will share in his horrid schemes. If I can convince him I *am* one, at least until our brothers arrive . . . that may be our best chance."

Idonia shook her head. "It's too dangerous. There is still some little time. I have supplies packed, I've drawn up a map. I can help you leave."

Liesl shook her head, smiling sadly. "It's already too late for that. Please, let me try this my way."

"I still have the daggers," I said, patting my sleeve. "I can stab him."

"I've seen him run through the chest with a sword," Idonia said, pressing her lips into a grim line. "He lived."

"Love will stay his hand," Liesl said. "I know it."

"Liesl," I said, taking her hand in mine. "Bluebeard knows only cruelty and selfish ambition. How can you think that will work?" And how would she pretend to love such a foul man, after all she knew?

She pushed a lock of hair behind my ear, looking at me in that way she sometimes does—the way that says I am too young and naïve to understand. "Even monsters want to be loved."

I pursed my lips, holding her gaze. She seemed far calmer than I expected. Perhaps there was a chance this would work. "Alright," I said. "Alright, we will try it your way. But if it doesn't work, I'm stabbing him."

Liesl laughed, a little huffing breath. "Very well. Now please, Idonia, we have been traveling half the day. Could you bring us tea to the library?"

Idonia blinked in surprise but then smoothed her hands over her apron and inclined her head. "Of course."

She left us, and Liesl led me up to the library. We did not bother to clean up or change—with so little life ahead of us, it hardly seemed worthwhile. I was speechless, desperately hoping she was right, that her words would convince her wicked husband.

The shattered window through which we'd made our escape had been boarded over, but the chessboard was still set up on the little table, the books sat snug in their shelves, the richly colored rug lay flat. There was some small comfort in the familiarity.

The scents of smoke and old books embraced me as I took my usual chair before the hearth. Liesl took hers while the servants stoked the fire and exchanged furtive glances. I wondered again how much they knew. Perhaps they could only sense that we were doomed or would meet whatever "curse" they thought fell upon the past mistresses of this house.

When they'd gone, and the fire was roaring, I asked Liesl how she could be so calm.

"I suppose this is what happens when you see your circumstances clearly," she said. "When you have no options left, so you take the one chance you still have."

"Liesl," I said. "Our brothers might still come."

"I pray they don't," she said. "They have no hope of defeating him."

"If they do—"

"It is up to us, Anne. I shall do my best, and I hope that even if I fail in my part, you will be spared."

A tear spilled down my cheek and I sniffled. "Do not say that, Liesl. I could not survive if—if you were to meet the same fate as . . ."

"You can and you will. But please, do not worry yourself—ah, here is Idonia with the tea. Idonia, please sit with us. Keep us company until the master arrives."

"Very well, mistress," Idonia said, placing the tea tray and pulling a chair close to the hearth. "Though I must again ask if you would like my assistance to be on your way."

"It will not be necessary," Liesl said coolly. "But I would love to hear more about your past, Idonia. Like these poisoning attempts?"

"None of that matters now," Idonia said, letting out a long breath. "It seems I have failed you girls, just as I have failed the others."

"Not all of them," I said, thinking of Minna, and she gave me a strange look.

"Please. The distraction would be a comfort." Only then did just a bit of uncertainty show through Liesl's mask, and I realized she was not quite so confident in her plan as she wanted us to believe.

"I have not told anyone of my history for years," Idonia said. "I am not quite sure where to begin."

"When did you come to the castle?" Liesl asked. "Start with that."

She gazed into the fire, settling back into her chair. "I came here with Rosalind, nearly thirty-five years ago. By now, I suppose you must realize that his lifespan is not that of an ordinary man's—so you will believe me when I say he had already been married four times by the time my lady agreed to marry him, though we did not know that then."

"Was she very much in love?" I asked.

Idonia smiled wryly. "Yes, but not with him. She and I loved each other dearly, passionately, but we did not know how we could be together. Even had I been a man, her rank was such that there never could have been an alliance between us. But Rosalind, she found a way. She married an old, widower nobleman and brought me with her to work on the castle staff.

"We were young then. We thought we could be happy together. At first, we were; you have seen how little time Bluebeard spends with his wives, and we had many hours to ourselves. But then strange events began to occur in her bedroom at night. She would have thought herself mad had I not been there to witness them—I suppose the same has happened to you, though I have done all I can to appease the ghosts."

Liesl and I nodded. I was enthralled by her story, hoping against logic that it might have a happier ending than I knew it must. Which of the distorted faces that will forever haunt my memories belonged to the woman Idonia had loved? And how had she stayed here so many years after what happened?

"Of course, that devil of a man tested my Rosalind just as he tested all the others. She did not tell me of the key or that she had looked until she had already done it, though I cannot say I would have stopped her if I'd known what she was to do. In any case, he returned and somehow knew what she had done, and he killed her too."

It had been so long, I supposed, that Idonia did not cry when she thought of it, though there was an undercurrent of pain beneath her steady words.

"You have seen the room beneath the castle, though I tried to hide it from you. I have not seen it myself, though my mistress described it to me, and I know the horrors it holds. I could not go down there after she was killed. I knew I would not survive the way I would blame myself, seeing her there."

"Why did you stay?" I asked, my voice small and strained.

"He told me she had run away," Idonia said, laughing bitterly. "I nearly told him all I knew of what she had seen, but before I could, he asked me to stay on the staff. He liked my work and thought I might take over someday for the housekeeper he had at the time, who was quite old. Often have I wondered if I did the wrong thing by staying—but I was deep in grief and had nowhere else to go. I thought perhaps if I did my job well, if I ran the estate and his events efficiently, he might not see the need for another wife, or at least it might delay him. And I knew that, if I were ever to have revenge, I could only get it by staying close to that devil."

"The poison garden," I whispered.

"Yes," she said. The fire made one side of her face glow and cast the other in shadows. "I'd always loved plants as much as my lady did—it is her garden that you and Sebastian have restored on the hill, and you've done a lovely job of it—so I knew of a few plants that might be slipped unnoticed into someone's drink. I started small, but he never became ill. I studied and grew more plants, eventually trying concoctions of several poisons together. He could not be invincible, or so I thought."

She shook her head, frowning at the memory. "My garden grew, as did my skill with the different poisons and plants, yet still he lived. I learned, too, that other accidents which may befall a person and take their life did no harm to him. Around that time, he began courting a new wife. As I had failed at preventing him taking another, I decided that my role here was not only about revenge but about saving the next young woman who should fall into his grasp."

"I hope I shall be the last," Liesl said.

"It had been so long since Amalie that I did not think there would be another," Idonia said. "I hoped that perhaps it was all behind me, and I might rest in my old age, though remaining ever vigilant for an opportunity to take my revenge for Rosalind. But then he brought you home. I poisoned his tea with everything I had. I know how severe I was on you both, but I know how hard it is to try to live among the upper class when you were not born to it. I tried to help you be the wife he wants, at least long enough for one of my poison mixtures to work."

She turned to me. "I was especially harsh with you, Anne. You reminded me so much of myself at that age. I tried to smooth out your manners so you might find a suitor to take you from the castle. You were so curious, always asking Cook and Sebastian about the past. I knew you must leave. And I tried to prevent either of you from going anywhere near that room."

I bit my lip, feeling guilty. If I had not been so suspicious of Idonia, would I have been so insistent that Liesl and I use the golden key? She might have returned it to Bluebeard, unused and unstained, and we never would have needed to run. But would it have been better for her to have been married, unknowing, to a killer? Was ignorant safety better than hideous truths laid bare?

Idonia gazed into the fire in silence for a few moments. When she spoke again, her voice was thick with emotion. "I do not want to lose you girls as well. Please, it is not too late; let me send you off."

"As I have said, it will not be necessary," Liesl said. "Thank you for sharing your story with us. If you don't mind, I would like to be alone with my sister now."

"Very well, mistress," Idonia said, standing and smoothing out her skirts. At the door, she turned once, looking back at us sitting calmly near the hearth as we have done so many other evenings here. I hope it will not be her last memory of us.

After she had gone, Liesl asked if I would record all we had learned in my diary.

"Why?" I asked. There seemed no point, as we would either be killed tonight or live long enough for me to record Idonia's conversation later.

"Just in case my plan fails," Liesl said, which was less than reassuring.

Once again, I have turned to this book and to writing all I know, and I suppose if these are to be my last hours, writing and comforting my sister is not the worst way I could have spent them. I am glad Liesl is here with me at the end.

I only wish I could have said goodbye to my family. I pray they will live long lives, free of the terrors that have shadowed ours. I also pray Minna and Hugo will be blessed for the help they gave us.

Why is it that in my last moments, I am thinking not only of my family and those who have helped us, but also of a pale, dark-haired boy who I once worked beside in the sunshine, before I had such fear and knew so many sinister secrets? I pray for him, too.

I wanted to face my end with a dry eye and my chin held up, but now the tears are falling, and I cannot stop them. Liesl is stronger than I. She sits tearless on a velvet sofa, gazing into the flickering candlelight. I only wish —

A horse just whinnied outside, making me drop my pen. Bluebeard has returned, and it is too late for so many things.

CHAPTER FIFTY-ONE

Letter from Klaus

18 OCTOBER

Anne,

I write again, though I do not know if my last letter has reached you or if this one shall. How I wish we were not on foot! We beg everyone we pass for use of their horses, but when they hear which castle we intend to ride them to, they will not oblige us.

We are so near now, we should arrive a few hours after nightfall. If you and Liesl are still safe, please do whatever you can to push through until we arrive. We will save you, my little Annie. I pray we are not too late.

Klaus

CHAPTER FIFTY-TWO

Anne's Diary

19 OCTOBER

Bluebeard came for us while we sat in the library. His great clomping boots sounded in the hall, and I had the urge to rip the boards from the window, bloodying my nails, and jump out again. But I stayed quiet, looking to Liesl for guidance. She had a plan. Perhaps it would work.

He burst into the room with two great hooks hung from his belt, like those from which the wives were hung beneath the castle, and I realized with horror that perhaps that is how we were to go—hung up and left to die, our blood slowly seeping down to join that of the others in the sticky pool on the floor.

But Liesl stood and reached her arms out to him as soon as she saw him. She smiled, her eyes wet with tears that had not been there moments before. "My love," she said.

I did my best to hide my disgust, but Bluebeard was not looking at me. He stopped just inside the room and said nothing.

"I have seen the wrong I have done," Liesl said, looking demurely at the rug. "I should never have disobeyed you. I wish that you might forgive me. We can be happy yet."

"You want only to save your skin," Bluebeard growled, stepping closer to her—it took only a few strides for him to reach her.

I backed against the boarded-over window, afraid, but Liesl didn't so much as flinch. Instead, she looked up at him from beneath her lashes and said, "Please, my liege." Then she knelt before him, taking one of his hands in both of hers. "Forgive me. I shall never disobey you again."

From where I stood, she was silhouetted against the fire and I could not see her expression. I did see Bluebeard's, though, and I was surprised to see his lifted brows, his slightly parted lips. It was an expression of hope. He wanted to believe Liesl.

Slowly, I took a few steps around the chairs toward Bluebeard. He did not notice, too enthralled by the plaintive look on Liesl's face, so I continued until I stood nearly behind him. Fruitless as my plan may be, I needed to be near him to execute it. Though, perhaps there was no need.

"It is too late," Bluebeard said, his tone steeped in sorrow. "Things cannot be as they were before."

"They can be better, my love," Liesl said breathlessly, a tear streaking her face and reflecting the firelight. "Now that I have seen your great power." She took one hand from his and lifted it toward his cheek. He knelt beside her so she could reach, and she ran her fingertips over his cheek and down his beard.

I slipped one of the daggers from the sleeve of my dress, its smooth handle fitting comfortably into my hand. His focus was still entirely on Liesl. Could I stab him while his back was turned? Minna had said he could not be killed this way . . . and if I did kill him, what then? We would survive, but what would I become?

Liesl's eyes flicked to me, and she shook her head ever so slightly.

But Bluebeard saw. He *saw*, and he turned and grabbed me. I managed to stab him once in the shoulder before he caught my wrist in his other hand. He bled, but he did not cry out. He didn't even flinch. Instead, he clamped my wrist in his hand, squeezing until I dropped the dagger to the floor. His eyes lit with fiery rage.

He tossed me against the wall as if I were a rag doll, knocking the wind from my chest, and turned on Liesl. "You dare deceive me, wife?"

Liesl somehow kept her voice steady and canted her chin toward him. "I did not deceive you. I want to join you—and I am sorry for my sister."

Catching my breath, I mustered enough control over myself to begin withdrawing the other dagger from my dress. But then Bluebeard picked up the one I'd dropped. His dark eyes glinted in the firelight.

"You want to join me in immortality?"

"Yes," Liesl said, a note of desperation entering her calm façade. "That is what I desire."

I cried out as he moved the dagger toward her, but instead of cutting or stabbing her, he pushed it into her palm.

"Begin now, then. Show you are loyal to me by starting down the path of immortality. Sacrifice your sister."

I gasped, but Liesl gazed at him, her steady mask only slipping in the form of widened eyes and beads of sweat on her forehead. She opened her mouth, but Bluebeard stopped her.

"Do not try to speak in her defense. She knows too much and is disloyal to us. She must die." He shoved her closer to me, and she caught her balance against the wall.

I'd finally slipped the dagger loose while she was distracted, but what use was it now? Liesl held the other, and I knew I could never use it on her.

"Do it," Bluebeard said. "Prove to me that you are worthy. That you are a better wife than any of those who came before."

Liesl held the blade, still slick with Bluebeard's blood, out in front of her. Her hands shook, and silent tears began to spill down her cheeks.

"Please," I pleaded. Because suddenly I was very afraid. Not of death, really, as I'd woken up each morning for the past week thinking that day would be my last. But that my sister did not really love me the way I'd always been sure she did. That she would not save me before anything else, that this had been her true plan. Perhaps the chasm between us really had opened this wide since we'd come to this accursed place. Despite all my efforts, I'd failed to protect her, so why should she protect me now? She might truly want *him* and everything he could offer her when forced to choose between us.

And then I realized that no matter what, I would choose her. Even here, even now.

"It's alright," I said. "Do it. Just . . . make it quick."

"What?" she asked breathlessly.

"If only one of us can leave this room alive, it should be you."

Bluebeard approached behind her, growling, "She's making it easy for you! Come, wife, I will guide your hand."

He moved her trembling wrist with his strong hand, angling the dagger closer to my throat. I swallowed, turned my chin up, and closed my eyes.

But then Liesl shrieked and turned on him. My eyes flew open, and I saw her slash across his belly, severing a chunk of his blue-black beard. He howled in pain and threw her aside as he had done to me only a few minutes ago.

I stared in dazed confusion for a heartbeat. Bluebeard hadn't reacted at all when I'd stabbed his shoulder, but a glancing cut to his belly caused severe pain? And then I realized what I needed to do.

All those times I'd caught him admiring his beard in the castle's mirrors. Minna's words: *it grows with the years even as the rest of him remains unchanging.* Even his name. It all pointed to the source of his power, and I felt foolish not to have seen it before.

Bluebeard and I got to our feet at the same time. Liesl was still sprawled on the floor, trying to recover from his blow.

I braced myself. There was no time to dwell on how killing a man—or a monster in the shape of a man—might change me. No time to doubt. This was not a tale from a book, and not all monsters could be defeated by being kind and true. My sister needed me to be brave and ruthless.

I hefted the dagger in my hand and lunged for Bluebeard.

He caught my wrist again, but instead of making me drop the dagger as he had before, he tried to force it back toward my own throat. I grunted, using all my strength to resist him, but I only managed to change his aim a little. The dagger glanced across my cheekbone before I could drop it. I cried out from the searing pain.

Liesl had managed to stand, and she struck Bluebeard with a heavy candelabra. It didn't hurt him, but it surprised him enough that he dropped me.

"Please," Liesl said, lowering her weapon. "We could be happy still. Leave my sister be, and I will do anything. I will be anyone you want. Please."

Bluebeard shook his head. "If only that were enough."

She'd made him pause long enough. The dagger, the one wet with my blood, was within reach. I slid its smooth handle into my palm. Then, with all the strength I had left in me, I launched myself up and grabbed his beard with my free hand. In one smooth motion, I sliced the dagger into his beard.

He cried out as if in horrible pain, though I drew no blood. I continued hacking through the black-blue beard until I'd severed it completely. His eyes, full of more shock than anger, met mine briefly. The strength left him, and he fell to his knees. A harsh, violent wind blew through the room, extinguishing the candles and whipping the curtains back and forth. As it grew stronger, it began to circle the room, flapping Liesl's and my skirts against our legs. Carried on it was the scent of wilting roses, the melancholy notes of a piano, and a striped owl's feather.

And then they joined us.

Six ghostly figures encircled Bluebeard where he knelt. Their forms were shadowy but unmistakably female. Those same women I had seen, their horror preserved by dark magic, in the depths of this castle. The eight of us together made a perfect ring surrounding Bluebeard. The wind died suddenly, leaving the room eerily still. Bluebeard's eyes flicked from figure to figure as their forms curled in the air like smoke. I realized with a chill that he recognized them—and yet I saw no remorse on his bloodless face.

The room grew cold and clammy as the ghosts arranged themselves, but I was not afraid. For the six faces that had haunted me these past nights were no longer masks of agony or fear or betrayal.

They were at peace.

One by one, the wives approached their bloodthirsty husband where he knelt, passing their wispy hands through his chest as if trying to pull out his heart. Then they would nod at Liesl, then me, with those serene expressions on their almost-faces, and dissipate into thin air. I only realized what they were doing when Bluebeard slowly began to fade away: they were taking back those bits of their spirits, the years he'd stolen from them.

By the time the fifth wife, Rosalind, took back her years, his hair and what was left of his beard had turned ash-white, and he fell sideways onto the rug in front of the hearth. She did not vanish after nodding to us, but instead floated off to a corner and watched the door. I had no time to wonder why, for then Amalie's spirit approached him.

She ran a hand over his cheek gently, then her other hand struck his chest, snakelike, and pulled. That was the end. He aged even further, then died and disintegrated into dust, and then to nothing, before our eyes.

When he'd vanished, along with Amalie's ghost, I finally dropped the dagger. The sound of it hitting the floor pulled us both back to reality, and I realized this was not a dream. Bluebeard was gone. We were safe.

Liesl fell to the floor, breathing heavily and sobbing. I scrambled over to her and took her in my arms.

"I would never hurt you—I wasn't going to, Anne, you must know—"

"*Shhh*," I said, smoothing her hair back. "I know. All is well. You did it."

"*We* did it," she said breathlessly. "It's over. It's really over."

I nodded, pulling her close. "They helped us. All along—this is what they wanted from us."

While Bluebeard was dying, I had been too distracted to notice the sounds at the door. But once I recovered my wits, I realized someone had been on the other side, trying to break it down. "Idonia!" I cried and hurried to open the door, which had blown shut with the ghostly wind.

"Thank the Lord," she said, relief playing out over her sharp features. She held the largest knife from the kitchens in her hands.

"You're both alive." Then she looked over my shoulder, toward the hearth. "But where is he?"

"He's dead," I said. "Or gone, at least." I pointed to the ring of keys and the pair of hooks on the floor, all that was left of him.

"How?" But then Idonia stilled, the color draining from her face. The knife she'd held clattered to the floor. The ghost in the corner had turned to face Idonia, was moving toward her . . .

I almost cried out, afraid she would do to Idonia what they had all done to Bluebeard. Liesl stood, too, though her legs were weak, and she had to catch herself on a chair.

But before either of us could stop her, Idonia reached both arms out to the ghost. "Rosalind. *My* Rosalind." The ghost entered her embrace, running the backs of her shadowy fingers against Idonia's cheek. Idonia's skin was wrinkled, but even through Rosalind's shifting, shadowy form, I could see that she appeared a young woman still. She was trapped by death in youth, robbed of the years that had etched lines into Idonia's skin.

Liesl and I exchanged a glance, but we said nothing. We would not have, for all the world.

"I never thought I'd see you again," Idonia whispered to her. "Are you at peace now?"

Something that might have been a smile crossed Rosalind's face.

But even as Idonia tried to stroke the smoky, silhouetted curls of Rosalind's hair, to touch that which had no physical form, Rosalind was fading away. It seemed it had taken some effort on her part to cling to this world long enough to see her lost love.

A solitary tear ran down Idonia's wrinkled cheek as Rosalind reached out with her wispy, flowing hands and squeezed Idonia's solid, work-roughened ones. Then the last ghost vanished from Tiefenwald Castle.

We all stood for a few moments in silence. Idonia swiped at her cheek and straightened her spine. She took a step, but her legs wobbled. Liesl and I went to her sides and helped her into one of the upholstered chairs in front of the hearth.

Idonia gazed at the great hooks, their black shapes casting shadows over the floral pattern of the rug in the firelight. "I was so afraid he would find me out. And then that I would die of old age before I could complete my vow. Before I could avenge my dear Rosalind." She took a deep, steadying breath, then looked us both in the eyes. "You were able to do what I could not, all of these years. How?"

Liesl tucked a blanket over Idonia's legs and nodded to me.

"It was his beard," I said. "I cut it, and he . . . " I trailed off, not wanting to remember the horrifying sight of him withering away before our eyes. Unsure how to explain what we'd just witnessed. "There were . . . spirits, too," I said. "After I cut his beard, the wives, they came and they . . . I think they took the years back from him. He aged before our eyes, then faded into nothing."

"I should have known," Idonia said. Then she looked up. "Did it pain him?"

I swallowed. "He cried out as if it did when I cut his beard, though I know I did not cut his flesh. And when the . . . spirits . . . each took something from him, he was too weak to cry out."

"No measure of pain would be enough to repay all that he has inflicted on others," Idonia said. "But I am glad to hear it nonetheless." She put her elbows on her knees and her face in her hands. "If only I had thought of his hideous blue beard," she said. "How much suffering might I have prevented?"

"You couldn't have known," Liesl said. She knelt beside Idonia's chair and took her hand. "And you have done what you could. We are alive. Minna is alive. Rosalind and the other wives, they are at peace now. We saw it."

She looked up from her hands. "Minna is alive?"

"Yes," I said. "She sheltered us when we escaped the castle. She is alive and well, and has a son. She survived, thanks to you."

Idonia's eyes welled with tears. Just then, shouts sounded outside. I sprang up and hurried to the window. My heart pounded and my fingers tingled with fear. Had Bluebeard returned, somehow, to take his revenge?

But it was a group of men carrying torches and farm implements—men I recognized. Our brothers and some village friends led by Klaus, and behind them, Sebastian. Come to save us, too late. The sight of those familiar, loved faces unlocked something in me. The horrible events and all the fear of the last few days rushed over me, and I joined Liesl in sobbing into Idonia's strong arms.

CHAPTER FIFTY-THREE

Letter from Liesl

20 OCTOBER

Dearest Mother,

I woke up so late this morning, it was nearly afternoon. I blinked away my sleep and realized two things. First was that, against all odds, Anne and I have survived our ordeal here at Tiefenwald Castle. Second, I've had my first full, restful night of sleep since leaving home, and I am nearly brought to tears with the relief of it. No fighting off fever, no more ghosts to torment me, no worries that my mind has come unhinged, no fleeing the wicked man I married. I suppose sleep is one of those things that we take for granted until we are without it.

I truly believe you were there yesterday, with your daughters and the ghosts of the wives, and saw this wicked man's long-overdue demise, so I will not recount it here. In any case, it still seems like something from a dream or a tale and not our lives in this world.

I'm left now with what to do next.

We must expose some of what Bluebeard has done—not the magic and blood-borne immortality, but the cruelty and murder. I shall look to Anne to spin the right tale of what happened. We could burn down this accursed place and start anew, or we could try to make a life here. I would be a rich widow with a vast estate at my disposal. Either way, the family will be secure. The future is ours to create.

I feel I do not deserve any of this, despite all we've been through. It was my mistake that brought us to this point, my foolishness and selfishness, my grasping at more than I was born to. Idonia says I'm being silly, and that if the estate was in the hands of an undeserving monster for so long, why shouldn't it be enjoyed by our family now? She has a point. Perhaps we could invite Minna and Hugo to live here as well, to reward them for helping us in our time of direst need.

Despite everything, I still have the same longing I always did, the one I hid away, even from myself, so that I could win a better life for those I love. If I can ever trust another man that way again, I want a husband. A true partner in life. I cannot help but think of Hugo. How kind, how honest and hardworking he was, how gentle with me when we walked in his pasture. If I dare marry again someday—and it is a long road ahead of me, if I choose that path—I hope it will be to someone like him.

Well, Mother. I must end here. There are a great many decisions to be made and matters to attend to. The first shall be the hardest and most gruesome, but you always taught me to address the most difficult task first. The poor wives before me must be laid to rest properly, and I shall see it done before another night falls upon the castle.

I still miss you more than words can say.

With all my love,

Liesl

CHAPTER FIFTY-FOUR

Anne's Diary

3 NOVEMBER

Liesl and I wanted to burn down the castle and with it, all its horrid memories.

Idonia said she would not stop us, but in the end, she convinced us to keep the castle instead. She said we had earned it, after the terrors and trials we had been through, and that it was time for this grand edifice to house people deserving of its beauty. "Your victory was hard-won," Idonia said. "You might as well enjoy what you can of its spoils."

We could not believe we deserved any such thing after all our foolishness and our narrow escape, but then Liesl had the idea to ask Minna and Hugo to come live in the castle with us, along with our father and our youngest brothers. The castle's many rooms shall be used once again, and we shall have people we love close to us once more. This might really become my home, and I will no longer feel the loneliness and homesickness of my first weeks here. Someday, Liesl and I might set up a school here and share the castle's wonderful library with anyone who wishes to learn.

Minna, at first, was afraid to return to the place that had so haunted her, but she wanted to pay her respects to Amalie as soon as possible. We buried the wives properly, in the garden on the hill. The fading black flowers now adorn their graves, and the sun rises over them every morning.

On the altar in that room, we found scrolls written by Bluebeard, describing his search for a partner in his twisted quest for immortality. I read them all, wanting to learn everything I could about the women who had lived here before. The women who, even after their own tragic and gruesome deaths, saved us.

There have been no more hauntings since we moved back to the castle, and after completing the sickening task of retrieving the wives' bodies, we sealed the room beneath the castle and vowed never to go near it again.

The story has spread through all of Bluebeard's acquaintances now. Not the true story, of course, which is known only to the few people we can trust with it, but the tale we spun, of Bluebeard growing ill and passing away, and after, our discovery of his dark secrets and what became of his missing wives. Many have sent their condolences or accounts of their shock or, worst of all, their assurances that they'd always had suspicions about my sister's dead husband. None of them seemed to regret enjoying his wealth, however, and a few even had the audacity to say they look forward to Liesl's next ball.

They shall be waiting a long time for their invitations.

There is no letter from Gustav among them, which is not surprising, but there is one from Franz. In it he apologized to me for his cowardice in not doing more to assist us when we were in need. He hopes I might forgive him one day, and that we shall be friends again. A small part of me wishes that we could, that I could dance and laugh with him, and forgive, but I am not the girl I once was.

I have seen a smallness, an ugliness, in him and in many others of the nobility—perhaps even in the world at large—and I cannot pretend it is not there. I have not written back to him, and I do not think I shall.

It is difficult to see beauty in the castle again after all that has happened to us, and after all I know that has happened before, but I am determined. Slowly, I am able to take in the craftsmanship of the carved wooden railing along the marble staircase, to enjoy the light spilling across the rug in the library in stained glass-tinted colors. Each day grows colder—we had our first snow a few days past—which makes the conservatory more magical. It is one of the few rooms in which I had never seen the monster my sister was once married to, so it remains untarnished.

And, of course, it reminds me of Sebastian.

In all the excitement at our brothers' arrival, I was not able to speak to him. I did see the relief on his features, and I knew then that he couldn't have known what Bluebeard truly was. In the days since, I have avoided him, which was no difficulty with everything that needed to be set right and the future Liesl and I had to plan.

But I cannot avoid him forever, especially as I remember thinking of him in what I believed to be my last moments. I had been hurt by our fight at the last ball, but perhaps he really had only been trying to protect me. After all, how different things might have been if I had accepted a proposal from Franz or Gustav before Bluebeard even left to "test" Liesl.

I decided to seek Sebastian out late this afternoon, in the fading daylight. I knew he would be in the garden we had made together.

He sat at the edge of the fountain amidst light swirls of snowflakes. When he saw me, he turned my way, and a slight smile tugged at his lips. He brushed snow off the ledge beside him, and I sat on the cold stone, suddenly shy.

"Idonia told me you were unharmed," he said. "But I am not sure I believed it until just now."

Unharmed. My mind snagged on that word. I had few visible wounds—my turned ankle, the cut on my face, and the scratches from our frantic night in the woods have mostly healed now—but I did not feel unharmed. Not at all.

I turned to look back at the castle, silhouetted as the sun began to sink beneath the horizon, and Sebastian inhaled sharply.

"What is it?" I asked, but his hand was already reaching for my face, for the ugly scar marring my cheek.

"'Unharmed' was the wrong word to use," he said, grimacing and shaking his head. "Idonia didn't tell me about this."

I took a step back from him and covered the scar with my hand. "When I tried to save Liesl, I tussled with Bluebeard. He had the dagger and . . . "

"I should have been here," Sebastian said, pain etched across his face and straining his voice. "I should have found a way."

"You did what you could," I said. "If you had been here, you might have been killed." My own voice was rough, and I feared it gave away how much I felt for him. We held each other's gaze for a heartbeat too long.

Sebastian's mouth tugged up into a half-smile. "You're so brave," he said. Gently, he pulled my hand from my scar and cupped my cheek in his hand, running his thumb along the silvery-pink slash. "You may not be unharmed, but I can see that you're as well as can be expected. When you've had more time to recover, you shall be quite as well as you were before."

His belief—that I could be myself again—twisted something inside me. It may have been hope, something I have been too afraid to indulge since the miracle of our survival. How can I believe he's really gone? I looked at the six graves among the snow-laden flowers. How could I know their souls were truly at peace now? Why should Liesl and I have a chance to be happy again when they do not?

"It gets better each day," I said, watching snowflakes descend upon my dark wool skirts.

Sebastian dropped his hand from my face and cleared his throat. "I wanted to apologize. I knew so little—I still know so little—of who Bluebeard really was, and I tried to warn you, but I went about it all wrong. I was afraid . . . when I left, I was afraid that I had hurt you, and that *he* would really hurt you while I was away, and that would have been the last thing—" He huffed out a long breath.

"I was hurt," I admitted. "I didn't understand why you pushed me away, and especially how you could say it was too late for Liesl."

"I did not want to, but I didn't see another way . . . " Sebastian shook his head. "If you, at least, could be saved, that would be something. Perhaps all I could do."

He laced his hands together. "I did not know what happened to the other wives, only that there had been others before. My father had hints from Amalie that she was in danger, and suspected her disappearance was no accident. He and Idonia helped Minna flee the castle, and Idonia told him a little of Bluebeard's pattern, though she vowed never to speak of it again after that night. From what he shared with me, I knew you and Liesl would not be safe here much longer."

"How could your father stay on here, suspecting such horrible things of his master?"

"That was just it—he only had suspicions, no proof of anything. I was only a toddler, and without my mother, he didn't know how to start again or leave his life's work behind. So he raised me here and always told me we would leave when I was grown. When he died, though, I found I couldn't leave all the memories of him. I didn't know where else to go. And I'd almost forgotten what he'd told me of Minna and Amalie until you and Liesl arrived."

I nodded, absently tracing patterns in the snow on the edge of the fountain. "It all worked out in the end, I suppose."

"Not everything," he said, his eyes fixed on mine.

My heart began to beat faster, and I had to look away. Despite the chill, my cheeks were burning.

"Anne," he said, leaning toward me. "I said several things I did not mean that night. I was so torn because I wanted you safe, but I also, selfishly, did not want you to go."

Slowly, I looked up at him again. White snowflakes were caught in his eyelashes and stood out against his black hair. We would be quite covered in snow soon if we stayed out much longer. "I did not want to go," I whispered. "I could not leave my sister, and I . . . wanted to be where you were."

"As did I," he said. "And I was so jealous to see you with those others, but then you danced with me. You danced with me, and everything changed. I felt things—a great many things, and I thought there might be a chance—" He shook his head. "But I knew it was better for you to leave."

"Is that where 'it could never have worked between us' came from?" I asked, unable to resist mentioning the words that had run through my mind so many times since then.

He leaned back, hands covering his eyes and sliding down his face. "I wish I hadn't said that. But yes, it was in part because I was worried for your safety and did not want to encourage you, in however small a way, to stay at the castle."

"And the other part?"

"The other part is obvious, is it not?"

When I said nothing, he stood and paced in front of the fountain, pausing to cup a snow-covered rose in his hand momentarily before turning back to me. "I'm a gardener," he said, as if that explained everything.

"I'm a goatherd," I said, standing and gesturing off to the lawn around the castle, where our goats and Minna and Hugo's sheep grazed together in the patches of ground not yet lost to the snow.

"Perhaps you were," he said, "but then your sister married nobility."

"And he's gone now. What does that matter?"

"The distance between us is even greater now," he said, though he took a step closer to me, making his statement ironic. "Your sister owns a massive estate, and I am in her employ, even if I'm now allowed at the upstairs dinner table and have been given a room far too fine for me in the castle."

"And she has invited a shepherd and his mother to live here, as well as our whole family of goatherds," I said.

In fact, I suspect Hugo might be living here for a while. He and Liesl have spent a great deal of time together since he and his mother came, and I believe she is slowly opening up to him thanks to his kindness and steady patience. This morning, I saw them walking the lawn where his sheep grazed, arm and arm. Her smile and the whole scene took my breath for a moment. I almost felt as if I'd gone back in time, to our own fields and animals, and Liesl's easy smiles.

I hope she has come through this ordeal with her heart intact so that she might keep it for herself or give it to someone else as she sees fit. And Hugo just might be a man worthy of her.

"Are you telling me there is some cause for hope?" Sebastian asked, taking yet another step toward me. The setting sun gave his skin warmth and lit his pale blue eyes from within.

"Perhaps," I said, half-smiling. Smiles come a little harder to me now, after the horrors I've escaped, but they still come. As does happiness, in unexpected bursts. After all the darkness I have seen, I know I could slide further into it if I let myself. Instead, I am holding joy fiercely and choosing love and light whenever I can.

Because of that, I think this will be my last entry for a while. Maybe someday, after the wounds heal over and the nightmares come more seldom, I'll pick up my quill again. Not to write of poison gardens and blood magic and murdered wives. And not of fairy tales with pure-hearted knights, vicious monsters, and clean-drawn lines of good and evil.

No, I hope to write of how genteel manners can hide unspeakable horrors. Of the price women pay for safety. Of the kind people, the people who will help you, who give whatever little they have in a world that's selfish and cruel. Of people in adventures of their own making, the unbreakable bonds between sisters, hardscrabble lives and bittersweet choices. And of how, even in the darkest times, there is always something worth clinging to, something good. The sun shines and the flowers grow, despite everything.

Back in the garden we made together, I took one more step, closing the space between Sebastian and me. His familiar scent overwhelmed me as his hand came to my cheek, warm despite the snow. My heart beat against my ribs. I tilted my head up and pressed my lips softly against his. His other hand found my waist and pulled me closer to him, and for one perfect moment, we were lost in each other.

Night had fallen, the stars winked through the clouds, and it was time to return to the castle. I would eat a delicious, hearty dinner by the cozy glow of the candles, talking and laughing with all the people I love. I shall be happy, and that happiness shall be all the greater for the terrors that came before it.

Acknowledgements

I'm so grateful to everyone who helped support me in this journey, without whom you would not be holding this book in your hands!

First, I want to thank my friends and family for their tireless support. My husband Ryan, in particular, I want to thank for encouraging me in all my writing and publishing endeavors.

Writer networks have been incredibly important to me in my writing and publishing journeys. In particular, I'd like to thank the Rochester MN Writers Group, the Mothman Stans critique group, and my Query Wenches for all of their help and support! Beta readers were also vital to improving and polishing this story, and I would like to thank A.R. Frederiksen, Rebecca Froehlich, Jessie Knutson, Lily Mehallick, Ruby Martinez, G.W. Prouse, Johanna Randle, Debra Seltzer, Tova Seltzer, Michelle Tang, and Olivia Woods for all their efforts to that end.

I'm also so grateful to my street team for helping me promote *The Bloody Key*. Thank you Elizabeth Bane, A.R. Frederiksen, Lauren Liem, Ruby Martinez, G.W. Prouse, Johanna Randle, Michelle Tang, and Olivia Woods for sharing this book so enthusiastically!

I'd also like to thank Vicky Brewster for her editing savvy, Elaine Ho for bringing Anne and Liesl to life in her gorgeous cover illustration, and Mallory Rock for putting the final Gothic touches on the cover design.

Finally, I'd like to thank whoever decided to include Bluebeard, a tale of minimal magic and many murdered wives, among the much happier tales in my illustrated childhood fairy tale book. The story both fascinated and horrified me as a child, stuck with me over the years, and ultimately inspired Anne and Liesl's story.

About the Author

L.J. Thomas is a writer of speculative fiction. A native of South Dakota, she now lives in Minnesota with her husband and adopted dog. She works as an engineer by day and writes by night. In her free time, she enjoys the great outdoors, traveling, reading, and daydreaming about other worlds.

Author's Note

Reviews are vital to the success of indie authors. If you enjoyed this novel (or even if you didn't), please consider leaving an honest review on Amazon, Goodreads, or your favorite book review website.

Let's Connect!

ljthomasbooks.com
Twitter: @ljthomasbooks
Instagram: @ljthomasbooks
Email: author@ljthomasbooks.com

Also By L.J. Thomas

We Survivors: A Story From After the End

Made in United States
North Haven, CT
18 December 2023

45935295R00181